A DARKER SHADE OF BROWN

Dedicated in memory of my mother, Mrs. Salome Jones, whose love, guidance and prayers welded together a close, loving and supportive family and to my brother, Apollo, who nurtured my creative spirit and often made sacrifices to assure I got the education that would help smooth life's path. I am also dedicating it to those teachers whose guidance inspired me: Mrs. Fannie Johnson Elam Riley, my fifth grade teacher; Mrs. Annette Hubbard Roberts, my twelfth grade English teacher and Dr. Emma Lou Thornborough, my favorite college professor.

Published in the United States by
Beckham Publications Group, Inc.

ISBN: 978-0-9802380-3-7
10 9 8 7 6 5 4 3 2 1

Library of Congress Cataloging-in-publication data: 2007909213

A DARKER SHADE OF BROWN

A Novel about
BROWN VS. BOARD OF EDUCATION TOPEKA

Ernest C. Jones

Silver Spring

ACKNOWLEDGMENTS

WRITING A NOVEL IS A CHALLENGING AND SOLITARY EXPERIENCE THE support of others is essential to completing the task with your sanity in tact. I want to thank the following people for their encouragement, guidance, technical support, and tolerance during my trying moments:

My Family
Mrs. Merneshey J. Oliver, my sister
W. Sam Jones, my brother
Aldore Collier, my nephew
Lawrence, Jr., Michael, and Cedric Oliver, my nephews
Denise Oliver, my niece

Barry Peckham, Clinton Alexander and Carl Jager, my friends

PART I-THE DECISION

1

May 18, 1954 was a Tuesday ablaze with promise in Smoky Mountain, Tennessee, about twenty miles northeast of Memphis. The sun was just beginning to creep up the horizon, exposing the pale blue sky of a clear spring morning. Smoke bellowed from chimneys of the wooden shotgun houses in this neighborhood of third generation descendants of slavery. Many had been sharecroppers and had been schooled no further than the eighth grade. To the north, south and east were exclusively white middle-class communities where families lived in one and two story brick or stone houses with landscaped lawns.

Inside the Morton's house, the smell of fried pork, baked bread, simmering grits and strong black coffee lured each member to a breakfast that promised to stick to their bones. Reggie's heart was already racing. He jumped into his pants and shirt, and rushed out the back door to the pile of chopped wood in the yard. He quickly loaded his arms with all he could carry and dashed inside and unloaded next to the black iron cooking stove where the logs would remain until his mother was ready to cook the next meal.

"Sit down Reggie and eat your breakfast. You've got plenty time to get to school," Mrs. Morton commanded. She had prepared him a plate filled with her hearty breakfast and placed the jug of sorghum molasses next to it as a special treat. Reggie, his heart racing, scarfed down all the food in a matter of seconds.

"So long, Mom," Reggie said as he quickly pushed his chair from the table. He looked to see if his older brother was ready to go and, seeing no sign of him, headed out the door alone, leaving his mother shaking her head wondering if he thought things would change overnight.

Miss Wright's classroom overlooked the tar-covered playground surrounding the sturdy three story brick building built around 1910 for the schooling of colored children. It sat on the highest hill in the neighborhood, overshadowing the Baptist, Methodist and the Sanctified churches that were built after the school.

The clock on the wall indicated it was ten after eight. Professor Washington, the school's principal, widely thought of as a man dedicated to dancing to the music of the city's white political boss, picked up his bell and began swinging it, warning the students that classes would begin in five minutes.

As the echo of the bell traveled through the halls, feet pounded from all directions. Young girls with shining faces had their plaited hair adorned with ribbons, while young boys sporting flat top hair cuts, starched shirts and blue jeans, rushed to claim their seats. Reggie was breathing heavily. He had run all the way from home. He wondered if Miss Wright had heard the news and if she would talk about it.

Yesterday they had discussed the articles on current events in their "Weekly Reader," so she might not spend any more time on things not in her plan for the day. There were a bundle of things to do in class before the end of the school year: administering the annual standardized test in reading comprehension; finishing the chapter on diagramming sentences; six more lessons in spelling and, of course, preparing for the end of school celebrations.

As the bell's echo faded, Miss Wright nodded; the students stood and their voices rose in unison,

"O beautiful for spacious skies, for amber waves of grain, for purple mountains majesties above the fruited plains! America! America! God sheds his grace on thee and crowns thy good with brotherhood from sea to shining sea!"

After a moment's pause, they recited,

"I pledge allegiance to the Flag of the United States of America, and to the Republic for which it stands: one Nation, indivisible with Liberty and Justice for all."

"Take your seats class," Miss Wright commanded, looking over her wire rim glasses. The screeching sound of chairs moving across wooden floors rose as all forty students struggled to stuff their belongings in the open drawer under the seats of their wooden desks. Finally situated, they sat upright facing the blackboard. The sunshine gleamed through the windows pasted with flowers cut from pastel sheets of paper during art class. Pictures of George Washington and Abraham Lincoln were hung over the blackboard,which had been washed the night before with a damp cloth that had left white streaks. A poster on the wall separating the classroom from the coatroom claimed, "Music is to the soul as food is to the body." It was surrounded by music notes cut from sturdy sheets of colorful paper.

Miss Wright opened her attendance book and without looking up began to call each student's name and waited for each to announce his or her presence. Reggie shifted in his seat as if a bunch of ants had crawled inside his pants. He wanted to raise his hand and ask the question, but was afraid to interfere with Miss Wright's routine. She might consider his boldness too "mannish" and scold him in front of the class.

The students began to reach for their tablets to report on home work assignments, but instead of asking for those reports, Miss Wright moved from around her desk, stood in front of the class with her arms folded and asked, "Can anyone tell me what milestone in American history occurred yesterday?" Reggie's hand shot up slicing the air with the force of a shinning sword. "Okay Reggie," she said.

He leaped out of his seat, his eyes glistening. When he began to speak, he almost stuttered. "Yesterday, the Supreme Court ruled that segregated schools were unconstitutional and all schools had to be integrated. That means we can go to any school we like." Reggie found the concept fascinating but it wasn't something he could easily imagine. Segregation was the way of life where he grew up. Even the school day was different. White students began the day at 8:00 and ended at 3:15 while Negro students began at 8:15 and ended at 3:30. Many Negro students had to walk through white neighborhoods to get to their schools and the extra fifteen minutes were supposed to give white students a chance to clear the areas and avoid any contact with Negroes and any possible fights that might break out. The strategy to keep them apart just added to a history of contempt Negroes had for whites while at the same time creating an envious curiosity of what they were really like. Reggie and his friends often talked about bloodying the noses of white boys if they ever got a chance. Yet in their homes and at school, the phrase, "That's How White Folks Do It" was often uttered as the standard of ideal behavior.

The people Reggie knew stood in awe of the classical concert artist, Marian Anderson, because she had mastered an art form associated with white culture while the gospel singer, Mahalia Jackson, was considered a "good down home singing sister." But Reggie had also heard his parents talk about how the Negroes shouted, hugged and kissed each other in exuberant celebration every time Joe Louis knocked out one of his white opponents.

"Very good Reggie," Miss Wright said. "However, class, the Supreme Court decision does not mean you will be able to enroll in a white school next fall. It will take a long time before the decision will be put into practice, 'with all deliberate speed,' as the justices had instructed But it does mean this is the beginning of a new era in American history and your children are not likely to experience school as you have."

Reggie was disappointed. After all the judges did say the decision should be carried out immediately and the Supreme Court is the final word on the law of the land. He was ready to make the change next fall. The rest of the morning Reggie was distracted and anxious. He wanted to find a more optimistic perspective than Miss Wright's. He knew she would be eligible to retire in a few years - a time none of the parents were looking forward to because she was known for her commitment to improving their children's lives. Reggie thought she was probably worried what integration would mean for her and afraid for what would happen to Negro kids if they did not have teachers like her who cared so much about their future.

Reggie and his friends used to say her gray hair, wrinkled skin and slowed pace came from years of trying to mold all the knuckleheads that had challenged her commitment to education. Miss Wright was the only child of parents who got no further than the fifth grade. Her father was the Elder of Trigg Avenue Pentecostal Church in North Smoky Mountain. He told her over and over as a child that education was the key to the liberation of the Negro. He also made it clear that no boy was good enough for his daughter. Skinny with short hair, and a broad, flat nose, unwanted attention from boys was never much of a problem. After years of dreaming that some boy would defy her father, she decided she would accept her father's dream for her.

Students would return year after year thanking her for her guidance and leave still wondering who gave her that diamond engagement ring she wore so proudly. They used to say if she was engaged it had been the longest engagement anyone had ever heard of. Some speculated maybe she found the ring or maybe it was an heirloom, but she wore it on the ring finger. The speculation came to an abrupt halt one day after Sadie Frazier, who shared a party line with the Wright family, picked up the telephone and wouldn't put it down after hearing Miss Wright discussing a situation with one of her friends.

Sadie was known as a gossip and a blabbermouth. Her husband said she never stopped talking even after she went to sleep. Sadie counted the minutes until she could get to the beauty shop to spill the whole story. As soon as Bessie, the beautician, wiped the soap from Sadie's face after washing her hair, Sadie said, "I got the story behind that engagement ring Miss Wright been wearing."

The way Sadie told it, while Miss Wright was at Columbia University in New York City working on her Masters degree after receiving her Bachelor's from Tennessee State, she met this man named Timothy Afusa. Miss Wright said that he was an only child and a descendent of royalty in his native Liberia. "He was six feet tall," Sadie imitated in her best teacher's voice, "very stately with deep dark skin and thick wooly curly hair. He walked with his head high as if it had been in a brace." He called Evelyn his African princess and changed her life. She began to have difficulty concentrating on her studies. She just wanted to be near Timothy and hear his praises and feel his touch. She became very conscious of her appearance and spent hours picking the right outfit and applying make up. This was all new to her. She became obsessive about what needed to be done to keep him. She even asked her mother, whose only advice was, "Be yourself, dear." And so Miss Wright said, "to be myself is to be absurd. I need to hold this man not lose him." During the second year at Columbia, Timothy proposed with a beautiful diamond ring and she accepted immediately. The wedding was planned for August after both received their degrees. Her father was skeptical but Timothy was a candidate for a Masters Degree and he was from Africa. These were credentials acceptable to Elder Wright.Timothy went home after graduation in May to break the news to his family. Evelyn wanted to go with him, but he thought it would be better if he went alone. The plan was for him to return in July, begin work and find an apartment. Evelyn returned to Smoky Mountain and began planning the wedding. It was the first time she and Timothy had been separated for more than a week since the first date. She felt lonely and was anxious for the day he would be all hers.

The letter came at the end of June. Timothy's family was enraged about his impending marriage. It defied their plans for him to teach in their village and marry an African woman. The family ties were such that Timothy did not have the will to defy his family, especially his authoritarian father. Evelyn was devastated. Elder Wright saw the work of the devil trying to destroy his only child. He described Timothy as "Satan's Disciple" and thanked God his baby did not get messed up with that devil. Evelyn swore never to take off her diamond ring. After many sleepless nights she decided to marry herself to her mission of educating young Negro kids to take their rightful place in a white dominated society.

"And that's the God's honest truth," Sadie said. "I don't know who she was talking to, but the woman just let it all out."

When the bell finally rang for lunch time, Reggie rushed to the cafeteria, ordered his hot dogs, French fries and chocolate milk and rushed to the table where his friends gathered each day. Arnold was already there. As Reggie approached, Arnold said, "Hey Reggie, you seemed all excited this morning when we were discussing the Supreme Court decision. Do you really want to go to school with crackers? You know they don't bathe like we do and you know what their hair smells like when it gets wet. Can you stand that on a daily basis? You won't catch me cavorting with white people, let alone sitting in a class with teachers who hate Negroes. Arnold had the olive tan skin and straight hair of his divorced parents. He lived with his mother, a very proud woman who cherished her black heritage. She worked as a cook in a whites only restaurant downtown. Arnold was her only child. She taught him, with exhausting energy, to be proud of his heritage and to be suspicious of white people. His father owned a barber shop and had very little contact with the family. He loved to tell people his great grandfather was white. If you spent at least ten minutes in his shop, you were bound to hear him refer to someone as "that lazy no good Nigger." If you spent the day, you would never hear him say a positive word about Negroes.

Before Reggie could respond to Arnold, Beverly, one of the smartest girls in her class, arrived at the table. "Are you guys trying to figure out which schools in Smoky Mountain will be integrated?" she asked, sitting down with her lunch tray. She spoke as if she were reading from a text. "My mother and father were discussing the Supreme Court decision last night. They thought it was going to change the country, but they wondered what it would do for Negro students in the long run. They wanted to know if integrated schools meant integrated faculties and if that did not happen, it could be bad news for Negro students without Negro role models. I already planned to go to an integrated college in the North, so it doesn't really matter to me unless Miss Wright is wrong about the time it will take to carry it out." Beverly could never be found without a book in her hand and she never missed an opportunity to extol the contributions women had made to society. She was thin, had dark brown skin and wore her hair in a pony tail. On the beauty scale she would be considered average. The words, "latest fashion," would have difficulty parting her lips. Her mother was a nurse and her father owned a construction company. He built an eight room brick house that his neighbors called "The Negro Castle" because his trucks and equipment were parked on the property next to the house, leaving the impression that the house was always under construction.

Most of those envious neighbors who lived in the rented shotgun houses took pride in their homes. They painted their houses. They swept their sidewalks. Come spring, flowers blossomed from yards and lawns. Hedges were treated like favorite pets. They were cut and trimmed almost weekly. The sound of a hand driven lawn mower was a familiar wake up call on Saturday mornings. The grass had to be cut and the hedges trimmed before it got too hot. At Christmas time many houses were decorated with sparkling colored light bulbs that were attached to the edges of roofs and others trailed down doors and accented windows. Glowing artificial Christmas trees could be seen in windows. The City would give prizes to the best decorated houses in the white communities, but not in the Negro neighborhoods; however, that didn't stop the Negroes from decorating their homes.

Late afternoons around sunset in spring & summer, families would come out on their porches and sway in their swings that hung from the ceilings. Individuals passing by would always exchange pleasant greetings. To do otherwise was considered an insult. If a child neglected to greet someone, the parent would be notified and the child would be disciplined about their poor manners. Corporal punishment was common in families. It was usually carried out with branches of a tree, the "switch", or a leather belt. On those summer days when the ninety plus temperatures lingered into the evening, bedtime would be delayed until the heat had been tamed by the cool night breeze. There was no air conditioning and window fans were a luxury.

The caterers, florists, construction contractors, mechanics and proprietors of restaurants, liquor stores, barber shops and beauty salons were considered the community's elite. However, neighbors of all classes tended to get along. They were even comfortable correcting each others' children if they misbehaved.

Just as the gang began to focus on their trays, Alfred arrived at the table sporting a smile. "What's up, Reggie? You look like you just got the news you scored at the third grade level on the state's standardized reading test. Don't tell me, Miss Wright shattered your dream for next fall. I bet you were having visions of white people surrounding you in your new school, loving teachers and embracing students opening their arms welcoming you into white heaven. Wake up Reggie, it's all a dream. There will be no welcoming white arms during the time we are in school, maybe for our grandchildren. As for me I'm going to remain in a Negro school and go on to a Negro college." Alfred's mother was a florist who worked out of her home. His father was a factory worker. They were proud of their black heritage but could often be heard correcting Alfred with that familiar phrase, "That's how white folks do it."

Reggie was disappointed. He felt out of step with his friends and somewhat ashamed of his enthusiasm for wanting to go to school with white people, but this was the kind of thing everybody had always said Negroes should be able to do. Had Arnold and Alfred been listening?

When the bell rang at 3:30 each class lined up in an orderly fashion and quietly marched to the exit closest to their classroom. The safety guards were the first to leave the building, charging ahead to their stations at busy intersections with red flags ready to alert traffic to stop and make way for students. Once outside students gathered in their various groups, fell into horseplay, laughed and chased each other until they reached the white neighborhood. Then the noises faded until they were back in the area where Negroes lived. Reggie joined his group of friends but remained distracted. He didn't think of himself as naïve about white people. He still couldn't wash from his memory that cold and drizzly January evening four years ago when he and his brother were hovering around the coal heater in the middle of the front room trying to keep warm while listening to Amos and Andy on the radio. Suddenly there was this thundering pound on the door followed by the threatening words, "Police, Police." Fear spread through the house, paralyzing the family. No one said a word. They looked towards the door. Reggie's mother rose from her rocking chair, put down the needle and thread she was using to patch some pants and moved to the door with a slow nervous pace. Standing in the doorway were two overweight policemen with ruddy skin, wearing ill-fitting uniforms. One had menacing eyes and the other a barrel chest and stomach held up by a belt tucked under it. Without identifying himself, the one with menacing eyes demanded, "Where is Doug Morton?"

"May I ask what you want with him?" Mrs. Morton answered as her voice began to crack.

"Don't get smart with me auntie, just point him out!" The policeman shouted.

Mrs. Morton did not reply. The cop with the menacing eyes pushed her aside, looked around the room, pointed to Doug and said, "Come with me boy."

"What's this about, son?" Mrs. Morton asked as she tried to regain her balance.

"I don't know." Doug responded angrily.

"Where are you taking my son? What has he done?" Mrs. Morton pleaded.

The policeman again shouted, "Don't interfere auntie or we will take you too!" He handcuffed Doug and led him out of the house.

Mrs. Morton followed, reaching for Doug. Mr. Morton tried to hold her in the house. Reggie stood in the door watching and calling the policemen sons of bitches, under his breath.

"Let's call Reverend Bailey!" Mrs. Morton had cried.

"Let's wait for a while and see what happens." Mr. Morton tried to portray strength through his nervous voice.

"They could kill him!" Mrs. Morton shouted. "Somebody needs to do something. What are we waiting for?"

"Calm down woman," Mr. Morton demanded. "You are going to work yourself into a stroke and then we will have to worry about you."

That night, Mrs. Morton paced the floor rubbing her hands together as tears rolled down her face. Mr. Morton puffed his pipe vigorously. Reggie pretended to be listening to the radio, but just sat up in the chair, silently swearing at the policemen.

The sound of a car coming to a stop in front of the house was heard. It had been four hours since Doug left and everybody's nerves were raw and ready to explode with the slightest touch. Every comment made during the time was uttered emphatically as if they were angry with each other. Doug began limping towards the house.

"It's Doug!" Reggie called-out.

Mrs. Morton grabbed him in a hug as he walked through the door. Mr. Morton let out a deep sigh and fell back in his chair. Doug's face was swollen and there was a cut on his bottom lip. Mrs. Morton took a warm towel and wiped the blood from his face and applied mercurochrome ointment to the open wounds.

"What happened?" Mr. Morton asked.

Doug said the police drove around the neighborhood and asked him to tell them where to find someone named Nathan. Each time he told them he didn't know any Nathan they hit him with their club and said, "Don't lie to me boy. You uppity Niggers think you can talk any way you want to white people. Well, this is a lesson to show you can't."

"Who the hell is Nathan?" Mr. Morton asked.

"I don't know and I don't know why they singled me out," Doug said.

"Don't lie to me, boy." Mr. Morton said

"I am not lying."

"Leave the boy alone," Mrs. Morton pleaded as she embraced her son.

The following day Mrs. Morton was hanging out her washings in the back yard when her neighbor, Melissa, stuck her head out the door and asked if she could borrow some scissors. Mrs. Morton responded that she would have to find them and would bring them over as soon as she did. When she walked through the door at Melissa's, she was greeted with the question, "What happened last night? I saw the police go in your house and come out with Doug. Is he still in jail or back home? Have you seen him since then?" Melissa made no attempt to take the scissors Mrs. Morton was offering.

"Doug's home, he has some bruises on his face, but otherwise he is all right. We don't know why they arrested him." Just as she was about to go into more details, there was a knock on the door. The muscles in Mrs. Morton's body tightened. She thought the police had returned. It was Mrs. Bradshaw, Melissa's white social worker, making one of her routine visits. Mrs. Morton attempted to leave, but Melissa's curiosity had gotten the best of her. She asked Mrs. Morton to stay.

The social worker read off her list of questions, determining if there was sufficient food in the house and if the children were getting free lunches at school and then she asked if there were any questions or concerns. Melissa, anxious to get back to Mrs. Morton, assured Mrs. Bradshaw that things were fine and that the children were taking their glass jars to school to get free orange juice in the middle of the morning and were getting the tokens from the principal for their free lunch. Pleased with Melissa's answers, Mrs. Bradshaw turned to Mrs. Morton and, as a courtesy, asked, "How are you, today?"What does she mean? I'm not on welfare, Mrs. Morton thought. However, the question had sparked her anger and the whole story rolled out. She didn't care who heard it. When she finished, Mrs. Bradshaw sat shaking her head. She told Mrs. Morton she would like to help her file a complaint with the Mayor's office if she would like. Mrs. Morton immediately responded,

"Yes, I would."

"We'll meet me tomorrow morning outside City Hall at ten."

For the first time since the incident Mrs. Morton felt some relief. She thanked Mrs. Bradshaw over and over and assured her she would be there. When Mr. Morton arrived home from work, she couldn't wait to tell him about Mrs. Bradshaw's offer. Mr. Morton grunted.

"Nothing will ever come of it, who ever heard of a white policeman being disciplined for something done to a Negro."

"Well, we have to try," Mrs. Morton snapped.

At 9:30 sharp the next morning Mrs. Morton arrived at City Hall. She stood across the street and watched as people went up and down the row of steps leading to the fortified doors of this Romanesque style building. They were all white. Her heart rate began to increase and her hands shook. She thought about what Mr. Morton had said and wondered if anyone would listen to her.

By 10:00 Mrs. Bradshaw had not arrived. Mrs. Morton began to feel anxious. At 10:15 she still had not arrived. Mrs. Morton started to feel angry and depressed and tears began to well in her eyes. She reached into her purse and pulled out a handkerchief. When she raised her head, she saw Mrs. Bradshaw getting out of her car. She quickly wiped her eyes and tried to put on a pleasant face. Mrs. Bradshaw apologized for being late. She said there was an automobile accident that held up traffic.

"No apology is necessary, Ma'am," Mrs. Morton said with bubbling relief.

"When we get in there, I am going to tell Mayor Sterling's assistant that we have a complaint to file against the police officers that were patrolling South Smoky Mountain last night around 7:30. I will then ask you to tell them exactly what happened. Take your time and try to remember everything. It is important they hear the whole story. Don't be afraid. I'll be there to see that they don't try to intimidate you. Are you ready? Do you have any questions?" Mrs. Bradshaw asked.

"Yes, Ma'am, I'm ready. I understand what you have been saying;" but beads of sweat began to form on Mrs. Morton's nose. She wanted to wipe them away but didn't want to bring attention to them. She was hoping Mrs. Bradshaw would turn away long enough to give her the chance, but the opportunity never came. It was irritating but she silently prayed, "Dear Lord help me get through this."

The policeman at the reception desk looked at the two of them, frowned, and asked if he could help them. Mrs. Bradshaw, in a commanding voice, said, "We would like to lodge a complaint about the conduct of two police officers in the south side of town last night." The policeman shook his head and, without uttering a word, pointed in the direction of another officer who was sitting at his desk having coffee and a donut while thumbing through a stack of papers. When they approached him, he leaned back in his chair and asked what he could do for them with a slight smile on his face.

Mrs. Bradshaw explained why they had come. Mrs. Morton was nervous but her anger from last night still seethed in her and she told the story orderly and without missing a point. The officer looked bored and never took notes and never asked any questions. When Mrs. Morton finished, she signed a piece of paper that stated the date, time, precinct and had a check off box labeled, "Complaints." The officer said that he would look into it.

Two weeks after filing the complaint there was no word from the mayor's office. Mrs. Bradshaw checked on the case constantly, but each time she inquired she was told they were still looking into it. Finally the mayor's aid told Mrs. Bradshaw the investigation was over and they couldn't confirm the story told by Mrs. Morton and the case was closed. He suggested a more productive use of her time would be to try to teach those niggers how to tell the truth when dealing with white people.

"What does that mean?" Mrs. Bradshaw asked

The aide just stared at her with a mischievous smile and said, "Excuse me lady. I have other matters to attend to."

Mrs. Bradshaw tightened her fist, pounded on his desk, looked him straight in the eyes and said, "A more productive use of your time would be to do your job of protecting all the taxpaying citizens of this community." Her body began trembling as she reached for her briefcase and walked out of his office.

She pondered over how to break the news to Mrs. Morton and give her hope. She walked around the park across from the mayor's office. After half an hour, it occurred to her they could try writing the governor and ask for his intervention and maybe he would take action. He needed to make up for failing to keep his promise to include money in the budget to keep the Negro school playgrounds open during the summer months. White schools had kept theirs open for the past three years and a load of petitions had been sent to him demanding the same for Negro schools, but with no results.

As Mrs. Bradshaw was driving to Mrs. Morton's, she glanced in the rear view mirror before changing lanes and could see that anger was still plastered all over her face. If this is the first thing Mrs. Morton sees, she thought, there is a good chance she won't hear anything I have to say. As her car came to a stop at a red light, she noticed an elderly Negro man holding the hand of a little girl as they walked across the street. Her mind drifted back to that day when she was ten years old, playing in the wooded area just outside her backyard when she had heard a man's angry voice coming out of the woods. She tiptoed in the direction of the voice until she could see the back of this stockily built white man with his pants curled around his ankles, exposing his underwear and pale white hairy legs. He was standing over a young Negro girl who appeared to be the same age that Mrs. Bradshaw was at the time. One of the man's large hands was holding his crotch while the other was beckoning the girl, who was pleading, "I can't do this. Please let me go"

He balled his fist, grabbed the girl around her neck and said, "Who do you think you are talking to! You do what I say!"

"No, no, " the girl cried as his fist landed time after time on her face until blood streamed down and her voice went silent. The man dropped her limp body to the ground and wiped his fist on her dress. He glanced in the direction where Mrs. Bradshaw was hiding and pulled up his pants. When he turned back, she tipped away as quickly as she could. Later, she thought of going back and helping the girl, but was afraid the man would still be there. The next day she got up enough nerves and returned to the area to see if the girl was laying there dead, but no one was there. At dinner that night her parents talked about a Negro girl found in the area near their home unconscious and near death. It must have been the work of some of the Negro hoodlums roaming the streets looking for trouble, they concluded. Mrs. Bradshaw wanted to tell what she witnessed, but was afraid the man might have seen her. If the police found out he did it, he would think she told them and might come after her. She asked her mother if she could go to the hospital to see the girl. Her mother rubbed her hair, hugged her and said, "No, no my dear, this is not something you should do. The doctors will take good care of the girl."

When Mrs. Bradshaw arrived at the house she took a deep breath before knocking. Mrs. Morton opened the door after just one knock. Her hands were shaking. She invited Mrs. Bradshaw in and offered her a seat. Before Mrs. Bradshaw could speak, Mrs. Morton asked, "Did they complete the investigation?"

"Yes, but you know criminal investigations are difficult. There has to be a lot of evidence before a charge is confirmed. They claimed the story was denied by the two policemen on duty that night and there were no other witnesses."

"They never talked to us or came to look at Doug or get his story," Mrs. Morton said.

Mrs. Bradshaw took a deep breath and said, "I think we should take our concern to the governor."

Mrs. Morton's response was quick and terse. "I don't think that would do any good. Governor Payton hasn't done a thing for Negroes, so I'm pretty sure he won't make an exception for my situation." She turned to Mrs. Bradshaw trying to camouflage her anger and said, "I really appreciate all your help; without you I don't think we would have filed the complaint in the first place." Mrs. Bradshaw put her arms around Mrs. Morton's shoulder and said, "Please call me if there is ever anything you think I can do." She realized Mrs. Morton was right about Governor Payton, especially in any dealings with the police. He had made public statements all over Tennessee about policemen abusing Negroes, but no investigations had occurred in the past four years.

As soon as the door closed behind Mrs. Bradshaw, Mrs. Morton wept.

Reggie's memory of his mother's tears caused his anger to resurface. To this day he still wanted to get revenge on those policemen. Searching for some solace, his mind suddenly drifted back to those summers in Mississippi at Uncle Ted's where they would sit on the porch at sundown after a day of chopping cotton in the hot sun and listen to stories about the struggles of the past. Aunt Ruby loved to tell the one about how Reggie's mother and father got to Smoky Mountain. She said they were sharecropping down in the Mississippi Delta with a Mr. Ladder, a mean old cracker she would call him. She said her sister used to say she wasn't sure whether Mr. Ladder could count or whether he just wanted to cheat them out of their pay. During the year he would extend credit to the family to purchase meal, flour, sugar and other staples they needed to run their households.

After harvest time, when Mr. Ladder had sold the cotton from that year's crop and the time came for him to pay the Mortons for their work, he would report that they owed him just about everything they earned. One year Mrs. Morton decided she was going to keep her own records and, sure enough, they proved that Mr. Ladder was wrong. She insisted to her husband that he go back and point out his mistakes. Mr. Morton approached Mr. Ladder and asked if he would look at the figures his wife had come up with about what they owned him because her figures were not the same as his.

Mr. Ladder was furious. "Who taught your wife how to count? Tell her to go back and check her own figures. Boy I've got a good mind to whip you."

"Nobody gonna whip me and get away with it," Mr. Morton shot back. Mr. Ladder seemed to have frozen in the spot where he was standing. According to the family legend, his mouth dropped open to his knees, his eyes glared like hot coals, and his hands closed into fists. There were several other white men around who witnessed the remark. They all stood in silence as Mr. Morton walked away. When Mr. Morton told his wife, she knew that the dispute with Mr. Ladder would not stop until her husband was dead. So in the middle of the night, they gathered as much of their belongings as they could, hitched the old mule to the wagon and went to their friend Leonard who drove them over to Smoky Mountain to Mr. Morton's aunt. A week later word came down that Mr. Ladder and a group of his friends came after Mr. Morton with guns and a rope the night after he left.

2

"HEY MOM. WHERE ARE YOU? I SMELL SOMETHING COOKING IN MY NOSE. What is it?"

"I'm in here, Reggie. I need you to go down to Mr. Bob's and get me some baking powder before you settle down."

"What are we having for dinner?"

"Never mind that. You'll see when it's ready. Now go ahead and tell Mr. Bob to put it on the book."

As Reggie walked to the store, he had to pass the Charles' house. They were sitting on their front porch enjoying the cool spring breeze. They had no children and were fond of using their parenting skills on those in the neighborhood. When Mr. Charles saw Reggie, he yelled-out, "What did you learn in school today, boy?"

"Nothing new," Reggie said.

"Well, were you listening to what your teachers were teaching you?"

A bit agitated, Reggie said, "Yes sir, I was." Reggie had not forgiven Mr. Charles for telling his parents about the time he caught him smoking with a group of his buddies in the alley next to the Charles' house and the whipping he got when the news reached his parents. He picked up his pace so he would be out of reach of Mr. Charles' voice when he hurled the next comment which Reggie was sure would come. As his pace moved into a trot, he approached the home of the Morgans, who were considered the intellectuals in the community. Mrs. Morgan was a teacher, her husband a mail carrier, her daughter a social worker and her son a teacher. The family relished their position in the community and was somewhat aloof, controlling any efforts to damage their image. Reggie thought of them as folks to imitate. Going to an integrated school would put him on their level. Actually, he declared it could outdo them because they had all been educated in Negro schools which the Supreme Court Decision had verified were not equal to white schools.

When Reggie entered the store, there were two white women standing around the check-out counter with bagged groceries accusing the Supreme Court's Chief Justice, Earl Warren, of being a traitor and a blasphemer of God's design for the human race. Mr. Bob said he wondered whether President Eisenhower would find a way to put an end to this travesty, the worst the South had experienced since the Civil War and the invasion of the carpetbaggers.

Reggie tried to avoid the agitated women. He didn't want to fall victim to their anger so he dashed down the far aisle looking for the baking powder. When Mr. Bob saw him, he yelled out, "What are you after, boy? Come over here where I can keep an eye on you."

Nervous and angry, Reggie walked near the counter to wait until Mr. Bob freed him to move. Luckily, the frustrated women continued their complaints as if Reggie were just another can of pork and beans. When they finally moved from the counter and walked out of the store, Reggie breathed a sigh of relief.

"What do you want, boy?"

"Mom sent me to get some baking powder."

"Go down the middle aisle towards the end on the left. You'll find it."

Reggie felt like lashing out at Mr. Bob, but he knew that the consequences of a smart remark would cause his family trouble, so he just took the baking powder and headed out. Walking home, Reggie was glad to see that that Mr. Charles had gone into his house.

When Reggie opened his door, he could smell smothered liver and immediately his digestive juices began to dance. "When will dinner be ready?" He asked.

"In about a half an hour if your father and brother are here by then. Take a tea cake. It will hold you."

"Mom, Miss Wright had us talking about that Supreme Court decision today. I was the one who answered the questions when she asked what milestone in history took place yesterday. She thought it was a great decision for the Negro race, but it was not going to happen soon. I don't understand why it will take a long time if the Supreme Court said it had to be done 'with all deliberate speed.'"

"I don't know why either unless the court wants to give hateful white folks a chance to find a way out of letting Negro students in their schools. The decision was just handed down yesterday. There are a lot of things that have to be worked out before you actually enter one of those schools: which one will you go to; how many Negroes will they let in at one time. But never mind Miss Wright, son, things have changed with that decision. You going to have opportunities your father and I never had. Once you begin going to school with white students, you goanna realize what we have always said, you are as good as they are. Your education is goanna put you up against them for the jobs they think we can't do. And most of all, you goanna show them that Negroes can learn as well as they can. I just hope you don't get too big for your britches and forget where you came from. I pray to the Lord I am around to see you grow to be the dignified man you are destined to be."

Mrs. Morton had been thinking all day about the decision. She concluded it was a blessing from God, but there would likely be a lot more suffering before integration was carried out, and her children could be victims of some of that suffering. She had no doubts white folks weren't about to go to bed at night and wake-up the next morning and start sitting down next to Negroes at PTA meeting and inviting them over for cake and tea.

Doug came careening into the kitchen from outside. "Hey Mom, when are we going to eat? I promised the guys I would meet them on the playground at four-thirty. I'm pitching today." Doug was in ninth grade, a fairly good athlete, an average student, and free of any ambition. He had pictures of Jackie Robinson, Joe

Louis and Sugar Ray Robinson plastered on the wall of the room he shared with Reggie but none of these seem to give him any motivation. Hanging on the corner with his friends, often referred to as hoodlums, was his favorite thing to do. Mr. and Mrs. Morton agonized many hours and days over what would become of Doug. He was too "mannish" and that often got him in trouble. Fair or unfair, his association with neighborhood hoodlums was probably why he got beaten up by the police. In a few years, Mr. Morton decide that Doug would join the Army and what he had not been able to accomplish, the Army would. Mrs. Morton shivered at the thought of one of her sons following in the footsteps of those Negroes who had died or had legs shot off in Korea.

"We can eat as soon as your father gets home, but have you forgotten it's your turn to wash the dishes?"

"No Mom, you got it wrong. It's Reggie's turn."

Reggie stepped out of the bathroom with his hand rolled into a fist raised over his head. "Don't try it, bird brain. This is Tuesday and that's always your day. I know you can't count or remember which day it is, but, good brother, I am more than willing to help you out."

"Okay, egghead, Mr. Know-it-all, when I loaned you that dime last week to pay for your ticket to the circus, you said you would do the dishes for me two times. This, egg head, is time number two. Sunday was time number one. Now who can't count?"

Reggie could feel his temper rising. There were many names he wanted to call Doug but all of them would land him a whipping with that switch his mother kept behind the stove. All he would have to do to get out of it, however, was cry. She couldn't bear hearing him cry. Doug would never cry. He would stand there in defiance until his mother got tired. Both of them, however, would do everything possible to dodge a whipping from their father. His bear sized hand would reach for the leather belt he was wearing and before the boys realized a whipping was coming, powerful lashes were landing on their backside. When they cried he would demand they dry up those tears or he would continue. Trying to stop crying was as painful as the lashes themselves. If they knew ahead of time he was going to whip them, they would put on two pair of pants.

Mrs. Morton turned from the stove, wiped her hands on her apron, placed them on her hips and looked at Reggie and then Doug.

"Okay, that's enough name calling around here. I don't know anything about your agreement, but I know the two of you had better work it out without any more of that language."

Doug smiled at Reggie as he anticipated his next move.

"Well, little brothers, you still owe me, so what's it goanna be? Pay up now or do the dishes." Reggie walked away without admitting anything. "I guess this means you concede," Doug yelled out.

Reggie said nothing.

"All right y'all, dinner is ready. You can come to the table," Mrs. Morton announced as she sat down the hot pan of biscuits next to the bowl of butter beans, mashed potatoes and smothered liver. As soon as the last word was out of her mouth, the family bounded exuberantly to the table. "Not so fast," Mrs. Morton commanded. "I need to bless this food before you dive in. Lord, we thank you for your many blessings. There are so many we can't name them all, but just let me say we are grateful for our health, Roy's job, the roof over our heads and that Supreme Court decision. Please guide us that we may see clearly your will in making that decision and touch white folk's hearts so they may accept your will." Mr. Morton cleared his throat signaling Mrs. Morton to end the prayer. "And God, we are thankful for this food we are about to receive, may it be a nourishment to our bodies in Jesus name, amen."

The ritual of passing food, minimal chewing and quick swallowing began in earnest. "Y'all eat like unfed Negroes. White folks take their time eating their food and talk to each other during the meal." Mrs. Morton said. Mr. Morton grunted. Reggie and Doug raised their heads from their plates and smiled, then resumed their pace. She decided to take matters into her hands and looked at her husband and asked, "Roy, did you sell any of those raffle tickets I gave you for the church building fund?"

Without looking up he said, "No, I forgot. All those Negroes at the plant wanted to talk about was the Supreme Court decision. You would think they had been asked to move to the front of the bus. Some of them now want to think they are as good as white folks. I got news for them. You won't see any Negroes going to school with white folks in our lifetime.

After seventeen years of marriage, Mrs. Morton had come to terms with her husband's attitude. She refused to let his cynicism make her blood pressure rise. At least he worked hard and took care of his family. He loved his children, though encouraging them was not one of his strengths. Much like his father, he was good at disciplining through fear of his belt. Like many of his peers at that time, he prided himself on his sexual power and his ability to discipline. Demonstrating caring emotions was for pursuing sexual conquest. Mrs. Morton understood this history and struggled to walk that fine line between helping her sons reach another level while maintaining respect for their father and the culture of the community.

"Roy, that decision has been on everybody's mind. I told Reggie it will change the way we've been living. If Negro children can get the same education as white kids, they will have opportunities you and I never dreamed of." Mr. Morton never took his eyes off his plate. He just grunted.

"Ain't no court decision going to change these crackers, at least not in my life time," He said.

3

As spring marched towards summer, end of school activities took center stage at Lincoln Elementary, Reggie's school. The annual contest for class king and queen was in full force. Boys and girls took to the streets knocking on doors asking for donations to support their drive to win the crowns. Reggie had come in second place the past year and was ready to give it one more try.

Winners were awarded a place on the school's float that would be in the Negro Cotton Carnival Parade riding down Main and Deal streets. All the high school bands participated; putting on their best shows for the crowds on the sidewalks. The city's adult Negro king and queen donned red and white cotton robes. The queen wore a sparkling tiara and the king a red and white crown. They would always lead the parade in some late-model convertible. There were floats from all the schools and some community groups.

This year Reggie would again lose the contest to represent his class, but he was selected to join a group of bicycle riders in front of the school's float, behind the band. That, he concluded, made him a prince at least. The parade ended on Deal Street where an amusement park had been set up for the celebration. There the Ferris wheel towered over everything as it rolled over and over with screaming riders. Beside the bouncing horses on the merry-go-round, the irritatingly loudmouthed announcer invited folks to come see the fat lady and the man with a tail. Children rushed to buy cotton candy and boys tried their hand at pitching balls to knock over bottles and win teddy bears for their girlfriends.

A week after the carnival, Reggie walked the school's hallways and heard the sound of students rehearsing their dance steps for "Guys and Dolls" or singing, "When Johnny Comes Marching Home Again." They were preparing for the annual extravaganza, a stage show where each class performed for the rest of the school. It was an opportunity for all the school "hams" to have their day. Reggie remembered the year he was scheduled to sing a solo, but the show was cut short before his turn. He was angry and pleaded with Mrs. Jones to let him go on. When she refused, he mumbled "damn" but she heard him and called Mrs. Morton. Reggie got a good scolding when he arrived home which served as his lasting memory of the extravaganza.

There was no announcement or rumor about integrating schools in the fall. Reggie fell into a summer routine cutting neighbors' lawns for pay. Saturday afternoon was movie time. He and his friends would walk to the Ace Theater where they would buy popcorn, junior mints and tootsie rolls; and spend the afternoon watching cartoons of Bugs Bunny and the Road Runner, or Tarzan and Superman movies.

When August verged on September, Reggie began hoping there would be a last minute announcement that he would be assigned to Longview, the white school closest to him. But it never came, and sadly he returned to Lincoln Elementary in the fall.

The next school year in Smoky Mountain sailed by without any noticeable movement towards integration. Reggie was frustrated. That summer, as he sat on his porch swing in a state of melancholy on a hot steamy day that August, thinking he was the only one who expected change to come quickly, Arnold charged up the steps breathing heavily and leaning forward. Reggie looked to see if someone was chasing him. Arnold threw down a copy of Jet Magazine with pictures of Emmett Till in his casket and said, "The suckers who did this ought to be torched to death like they did him. I wish I had a gun. I would track them down, make them crawl and beg for their lives and then let them have one bullet every ten minutes."

Reggie looked at the pictures, placed his head in his hands and said, "I would be right there beside you."

As Reggie understood the story, Emmett Till was only fourteen years old and had journeyed from Chicago to Mississippi to visit his relatives when he was accused of whistling at a white woman in a store. A couple of days later, in the middle of the night, he was taken from his uncle's house by the owner of the store and the owner's brother in law. Three days later his body was found in a river. One eye was gouged out and his head was crushed in with a bullet hole.

Pictures of Emmett in the casket began showing up in all the newspapers and magazines. It outraged the country – Negroes and whites. There was an outcry for justice to be done. Reggie followed the story with horror as the two men were identified at their trial by Emmett Till's uncle, but were still acquitted of the charges.

There was a rumor a few weeks after the acquittal that the men were seen in a parking lot in downtown Smoky Mountain. Reggie and Arnold thought that this was their chance. On the Morton's porch again, they discussed buying switch blades, rushing to the lot, waiting for the men to return for their car. Then they would stare them down hoping to provoke a fight. Mrs. Morton overheard the conversation, rushed over and grabbed them both by the neck and shouted, "Are you out of your mind? I don't want to hear any more talk like this. Don't you know you could be killed just like that boy?" She released them from her grip and slapped them on their heads.

She broke out in a cold sweat just thinking about what could happen to them if they tried such a thing.

Labor Day, 1955, came and passed. It still didn't look like integration of schools in the Southern states was coming. White groups were developing strategies to set up private schools to counter the Supreme Court decision. White elected officials were publicly vowing they would not comply with it. San Antonio and Brownsville, Texas, were the only places that had complied with the law without strong resistance.

It became clear to Reggie his destination was Booker T. Washington High School, the first all Negro school built in Smoky Mountain. Doug was a sophomore there. Reggie's disappointment about his schooling overshadowed his anger over the murder of Emmett Till. Besides, things in Tennessee were never as bad as they were in Mississippi, he concluded

Shortly after school started, the Brooklyn Dodgers and Jackie Robinson won the World Series and Reggie got caught up in the hoopla and racial pride brought on by the victory. He joined the other students shouting and running through the halls hugging each other without objections from the teachers. Negroes on the streets greeted each other with, "How about our Jackie Robinson?" Reggie melted into life at Booker T. Washington. It was, after all, the premier high school in the city for Negroes and many of the well know families sent their children there and Reggie was getting all 'A's.

One day in early December Reggie arrived from school to find his mother almost hysterical. "Son I think the Lord is moving us another step forward. Now the Negroes down in Alabama have vowed to boycott the buses until they are allowed to sit wherever they want. A woman named Rosa Parks got on a bus in Montgomery sat in the white section and refused to get up and give a white man her seat."

"Well, I hope it doesn't take as long to integrate the buses in Alabama as it is taking to integrate the schools in Smoky Mountain," Reggie said.

"I do too, son. But there's this powerful preacher over there named Martin Luther King, Jr. leading the boycott. I believe there ain't no turning back now until these segregation laws are declared unlawful. Thank the Lord."

4

At Booker T. Washington Reggie found himself to be very popular and was considered among the brightest students in his class. On top of it all he won the heart of Mona Townsend, one of the most attractive girls at school. He first set his eyes on her in Civics class during freshman year. She had long black hair that reached down the middle of her back, an olive brown complexion, thin lips and a body shaped like a Coca Cola bottle. She received good grades, but students said it was more a reflection of her looks than her brain power. There was a feeling around the school that anyone with her features was destined for good grades and any girl with short hair, dark skin, and large lips had to be a genius if she wanted good grades. Mona's father was a doctor and her mother was an elementary school teacher. Reggie couldn't believe his luck. She was the dream of many boys on campus and Reggie couldn't believe he had won her heart considering he was not an athlete, which usually had their pick of the crop among the foxiest chicks. He had dark brown skin and was around five feet and eight. In the world of looks there was nothing outstanding about him. But he was out-going, smart with a sense of humor and a certain amount of humbleness.

Mona's parents were wary of Reggie because of his complexion and his family background. The Townsends foresaw their daughter's wedding day as the crowning point of years spent cultivating a light skinned princess who happened to be a Negro. She was their only child and their only opportunity to perpetuate the proud Townsend lineage. They especially did not want dark skinned grandchildren. After three years of referring to Reggie as, "that young man" and never inviting him to their home Mona still remained devoted to him. The Townsends decided on a plan to free their daughter. They would send her to a college that they were sure the Mortons could not afford. Once there, she would meet people with backgrounds more in keeping with her own and would forget all about Reggie.

Mrs. Morton wasn't exactly elated about Mona claiming her son as her own. She saw the relationship as nothing more than Mona's rebellion against her parents. She wondered what effect the day of reckoning would have on Reggie when Mona's real motive was revealed.

"That's my boy." Mr. Morton would say secretly. "He's got that Morton touch that women can't resist. He must have given it to her and she can't stop coming back for more. He'll show those uppity Niggers where their powers end."

5

THE END OF THE SCHOOL YEAR SAW DOUG ORDERING HIS CAP AND GOWN for graduation. In many ways Doug had stood in the shadow of his younger brother. He was on the football team but never became a star player. Girls found him attractive, but they would pull away after only short encounters. He had a low threshold for irritation and would become defensive at any perceived insult. Much to the chagrin of his mother, and the delight of his father, Doug decided to join the Army as soon as he graduated. Mrs. Morton had heard of a few Negro soldiers who had returned from Korea and were completing their education with government help but she feared Doug might return home in a box with a meaningless medal on his chest.

"Reggie, wait-up. Aren't you heading for Harlem House? Beverly and Alfred are already there." Arnold called-out. "Yeah, I'm on my way over there; but I'm supposed to meet Mona. As a matter of fact, I'm late", Reggie said. Reggie ran up the stairs of Harlem House huffing and puffing. Harlem House, a sundry that sold some of the best hot dogs in the city, was the favorite gathering place for kids in the neighborhood and one of the few that got their parents' approval. Five red leather stools were bolted along the counter and six booths lined up against the wall. Pictures of Joe Louis, Jackie Robinson, Nat King Cole, Booker T. Washington, Marian Anderson, Ethel Waters, Lena Horn, and Dorothy Dandridge adorned the walls. Mr. Snow, the owner, often referred to the heroes when counseling the kids about working hard and not giving up in the face of obstacles. He welcomed groups of teenagers in his place as long as they behaved themselves and spent money. He would always inquire about their future plans and was quick to offer advice on any subject. Often, the wrinkles in his face would become prominent, his eyes would squint and he would say, "When I was your age, I had to walk ten miles to the one room school house with a biscuit and a piece of fat-back for lunch. Life is too easy for you youngsters".

"Hey Reggie," called Beverly. "I'm surprised to see you here alone. Where is your other half?"

"If you mean Mona she is supposed to meet me here. As a matter of fact, she should be here now." Reggie sat down and they began to talk about school. Every few seconds Reggie looked towards the door, ignoring Beverly's sarcastic comment. Beverly and Arnold were not exactly fond of Mona. They considered her a high yellow "Siddity" society girl who thought she was better than them. Reggie was the darkest-skinned person they had ever seen her with. Mona sensed their distrust and kept her distance.

"So I've decided to apply to Howard University in Washington D.C. and Hampton in Newport News, Virginia," Arnold announced. "The one that accepts me and offers the highest scholarship is where I'll go. I'm hoping its Howard because I hear they got a lot more women than men up in Washington."

Beverly frowned, turned up her nose and said, "I don't think they give scholarships for sex lives."

Reggie looked again towards the door.

Before Arnold had a chance to respond, Beverly announced that her counselor, Mr. Sam Jones, had suggested she apply to Lakeland College in Brayer, Minnesota. He knew it was an excellent school and they were interested in attracting Negro students and she could easily get a scholarship considering her grades.

"Well, I hope you don't go up to lily white Minnesota and get knocked up by some white cat," Arnold blurted out.

"That's not in the cards. It would interfere with my goal of becoming the first Negro to sit on the Supreme Court."

"In what country? Haiti?" Arnold cracked, leaning back with a smirk on his face.

Alfred looked at Reggie and asked, "What are your plans?"

"Still working on it," Reggie said. He did not feel like defending his dream of going to an integrated school.

The door of the sundry swung open and Mona walked in. Reggie quickly jumped up and went to greet her. She seemed distressed and asked Reggie if they could go for a walk. Reggie nodded and looked towards the table where his friends were sitting and told them he was leaving. They nodded back in unison, winked and waved him good bye.

"Is everything okay?" Reggie asked.

"My father was just telling me his plans. He announced Daniel Shelton, Dr. Shelton's son, would be my escort for the debutante ball and asked me to apply to Barnard College in New York."

Reggie felt blood flush from his face and a knot rising in his stomach.

"It looks like he is trying to put the slip on me."

"Well, it won't work. If they want me to go through with that debutante stuff, you are going to be my escort. What about college, Reggie? Have you decided yet?"

Reggie was still trying to absorb the shock. He visualized Mona with some rich high yellow cat smiling and waving him good-bye and Arnold, Alfred and Beverly laughing at him.

"I'm not sure. What did you say to your father?"

"I told him I have plans of my own and he needed to hear mine before going off with his master plan."

"And what did he say?"

"He said he and Mother were only trying to make life as easy as possible for me."

"What did your mother say?"

"As usual she said nothing. I told them I had a date and walked out."

"I thought we would go to the same school," Reggie lamented. "And if we couldn't, I was hoping we would not be that far apart. If you go to New York, you'll forget about me."

"Reggie I could never forget about you no matter where I go and I don't want to be that far from you either. We have some time before applications are due. Let's develop our own plan. You really should begin deciding where you want to apply.

Mona resented her father for making plans without consulting her, but the thought of being in New York was exciting. She pictured the Fifth Avenue shops, Broadway, Radio City, movie stars and a town full of sophisticated people; however, she figured Barnard would never accept her. She and Reggie walked holding hands without talking for the next couple of minutes. Reggie broke the silence with another concern that was weighing heavily on him.

"What would I have to do if I am your escort for the debutante ball?"

"You will have to go to rehearsals with me leading up to the ball and of course the night of the ball you will escort me to the stage and later dance with me. You will be taught everything. There's nothing to it. You will see."

He was thinking that maybe he should let Daniel Shelton be her escort, as long as he doesn't kiss her. One mistake was all Dr. Townsend would need to show Mona that he was not for her. He kissed Mona on the cheek and continued home, his head was spinning with uncertainty.

Reggie's senior year was filled with a series of social events. There was the annual homecoming football game where seniors arrived in new fall fashions and paraded up and down the bleachers during half time. The game was just a side show. Reggie couldn't claim the latest fashion, but the chick on his arm said more than his clothes ever could.

In the middle of March, class rings arrived and seniors greeted them as if they represented induction into a secret society. Sweethearts anxiously waited to wear their boyfriend's ring on a chain around their necks. Some of the boys had dilemmas. They didn't want to make commitments or reveal the top girl on their list before announcing their date for the prom, the most important social event of the senior year but Reggie, after admiring it for an hour, gave his to Mona.

The Honor Society Boat Ride, an exclusive only for straight A students with high moral character and their dates, turned out to be a romantic evening. The ferry, encased in bright lights, chucked down the dark river at dusk with Smoky Mountain's skyline in the background and a full moon hovering above. The cool spring breeze produced a tranquilizing effect. Flashbulbs snapped, taunting the darkness. Reggie and Mona stood at the front of the boat holding hands enjoying the wind that swept across their faces. Reggie held onto her around the waist and confessed his love and his doubts about the future. Mona said she would always be with him. They both had to fight their pounding physical desires. The fear of disgrace and the lack of opportunity made that fight a little easier.

Mona won the battle over who would escort her to the debutante's ball. On that night, Mr. Morton dropped Reggie off at the Townsends. Reggie could feel the sweat gathering under his arms and a weakness in his knees. He took a deep breath and pushed the door bell. Mrs. Townsend greeted him and admired how he looked in his tuxedo. Dr. Townsend shook his hand firmly and invited him to sit while they waited for Mona. He asked Reggie if he had any questions about what was expected of him. Reggie assured him he remembers the lessons. Mrs. Townsend told Reggie there was nothing to be afraid of, which only made Reggie more nervous. Mona descended the stairs in a long white gown that accentuated her tan complexion and black hair. She reminded Reggie of Dorothy Dandridge in the role of Carmen Jones. Reggie forgot that he was nervous at that moment; he only felt proud.

The evening went without a flaw. Reggie relaxed after escorting Mona to the stage. When the time came for him to dance with her, he felt like a prince. Everybody in attendance was cordial, but not friendly. Most of the people he was introduced to directed their conversation to Mona after shaking his hand. He didn't care. He hadn't made any mistakes.

After the Debutante's ball, prom night was anticlimactic, except Dr. Townsend drove Reggie and Mona to and from the dance. However, the night was one to remember. They joined the other boys dressed in white jackets, black trousers and a cummerbund; girls in long gowns and wrist corsages. They glided across the floor of the gym doing the Cha Cha Cha, the jitterbug and the two-step slow dance under the watchful eyes of the stern face chaperones.

6

MONA HAD GONE AHEAD AND APPLIED TO BARNARD, BUT SHE AND REGGIE also applied to Davis State University, which had been for white students only before the Brown Decision. Mr. Sam Jones had helped Reggie complete his application for admission and a scholarship. Both Mona and Reggie's letters of acceptance from Davis arrived in the middle of April. Reggie's financial aid package gave him tuition and room and board, provided he maintained a "B" average. Reggie couldn't contain himself. His suppressed desire to go to an integrated school finally exploded. He felt proud, important, and reassured that dreams could come true. He was about to see first hand how white folks do it. The dream was even sweeter since Mona was also accepted. They hugged and kissed and Reggie said he was the happiest man on earth. Mona thought she would be more excited. She didn't realize until then the strength of her suppressed fantasy of living in New York. She began to feel anxious about whether she would be accepted at Barnard and guilty that she felt that way.

About three weeks after Mona received notice of her acceptance at Davis, the letter from Barnard arrived. Mrs. Townsend telephoned Dr. Townsend immediately and he insisted that she open it. He desperately wanted to know if his plan had worked. The medical director at the hospital where he practiced considered himself a mentor for Dr. Townsend. When he heard Dr. Townsend's daughter had applied to Barnard, he offered to assist in her application process. He told Dr. Townsend that his wife was a prominent fundraiser for Barnard and he would see what he could do. Dr. Townsend took the clue and unbeknownst to his family, he secretly shelled out a hundred dollars and prayed it was sufficient. It was all he could afford and Lord knows it would be worth every penny if Mona got admitted, he concluded.

Mrs. Townsend objected to opening the letter, but her husband's angry insistence was more powerful than her sense of privacy. The news of Mona's acceptance sent a bolt of joy through Dr. Townsend that he hadn't felt since waking up on Christmas morning when he was a child. He instructed his wife to hold the letter for him to give to Mona. At dinner that evening, between the main course and dessert he handed the letter across the table to Mona and said,

"This is the best news we have received in more years than I can remember. Barnard is one of the most prestigious schools for women in the world. You are lucky. You are going to have a chance to meet interesting and important people. There aren't many Negroes who get that chance."

"You opened my mail! What about respecting my privacy? Don't I have any rights around here?" Mona shouted and stormed from the table, squeezing the letter in her hand.

"It's time for you to grow up young lady," Dr. Townsend shouted after her.

In the quiet of her room, Mona dropped the letter on the desk and there starring back at her was Reggie's picture. Tears began to well in her eyes as she thought of breaking the news to him.

On the last day of Senior Week as they were walking home from graduation rehearsal, Reggie asked Mona if she had received any further mail from Davis about freshman week. Mona hesitated. She felt a knot in her stomach and her tongue seemed to thicken. She knew this was the moment of truth and she hadn't rehearsed her answer. When she hesitated, Reggie turned to face her and started to repeat the question.

Before he could say anything, Mona whispered, "I'm not going to be able to go to Davis. I was accepted at Barnard and my father insists that I go there."

Reggie felt dizzy. "How long have you known this?" he asked after releasing a deep breath he had taken to remain conscious.

"About a week." She didn't want to tell him exactly how long it had been. With tears streaming down her face, she immediately began a counter-strategy. "Reggie, it's not like I'm being banished to the other side of the world. I'll be home for all the holidays and the summers and I will write you all the time. We can make this work. I love you."

Reggie looked into Mona's eyes. She reached over and pulled him close and hugged him tightly.

"I don't know what it will be like not having you around everyday," Reggie said.

Mona exhaled and her shoulders slumped.

There were a flood of thoughts running through Reggie's mind as he left Mona. He wanted to believe their love would last, but his long held doubts about holding on to her surfaced. He was certain this was a victory for her parents. He tried to pacify himself by reminding himself that Barnard was a woman's college.

PART II - THE JOURNEY

7

Choking fumes from the Greyhound bus maneuvering into its designated parking space overwhelmed the line of waiting passengers on the dimly lit platform. Some coughed; some wiped their eyes, while others held their noses. Reggie stood stoically and kept his eyes on the suitcase his mother bought from the Goodwill. The suitcase told a truth about him that he wasn't ready to reveal to new people, but what was inside told a different story. His only regret was that he didn't have the tailor-made pants, now folded neatly in the suitcase, for the homecoming game when he could have showed off like the other students. But now he would be able to show white students he had style.

Reggie boarded the bus and headed for the back. He took a seat next to the window and exhaled. The adrenalin that had been pumping in his body since the day before was beginning to wear off, leaving him exhausted. He slumped back, closed his eyes, and began to slow down his breathing.

Yesterday the gang met at Harlem House and said their good byes. Arnold was going to Howard University in Washington – his first choice; Beverly was headed for Lakeland College in Minnesota and Alfred was staying close to home and attending Lane College. Everybody was excited about their new adventure and there was no criticism or jokes about Reggie's choice. Beverly was considered the real winner because she was going to college in the North. Rev. Bailey's message at the baccalaureate service was that they would face great challenges as they left their communities and entered the larger world, but "If you can take it you can make it" was his message. He reminded those going on to college that many of them would be the first generation in their families to do so and that would require them to pave the way for those coming after. He concluded his sermon by saying, "Whatever your future, the preparation given you at Booker T. Washington and the nurturing you have received from your parents and neighbors have given you the foundation to take it and make it."

Mr. Ball, the white superintendent of schools, paused at one point during his graduation speech as he looked over the class of the graduates. He finally said, "You students," but they swore he was about to say, "you niggers."

Reggie was number five in a class of three hundred fifty and his friends told him they would vote for him when he ran for president.

Reggie already missed his friends and began to wonder what Christmas would be like when they were all together again. He wondered what it would be like if Mona were still around. She had left for Barnard a week earlier and her first letter had already arrived. He reached into the brown bag his mother had prepared for his trip, shoving aside the securely wrapped fried chicken, slices of loaf bread, sweet potato pie and tea cakes until his hand felt the envelope. He pulled out the letter and read it again. She had arrived safely in New York and was trying to adjust to a college in the middle of the city. Her roommate was a white girl named Ellen Sawyer from Westport, Connecticut. The two hit it off immediately. The Sawyer family had been in New England since the 1700s. She had already traveled extensively in Europe and Africa with her parents and had gone to a boarding school with a few wealthy Negroes. Mona said that Ellen loved New York and was excited about exploring the city. Reggie sensed Mona was as excited about New York as Ellen but was down-playing her excitement for the sake of his feelings. She told him how much she missed him and she looked forward to Christmas.

Reggie remembered his father was edgy on graduation day and kept telling everybody to hurry up so they would not be late. He had squeezed Reggie's hand after the ceremony but said nothing. His mother couldn't stop hugging him. Somewhere in the middle of retracing those warm memories of the last few days, he drifted off to sleep.

When he awoke, the bus was racing down the highway. As he looked out the window, he noticed how fast the images on the landscape came into and then disappeared from view. It was sobering. He began wondering if he would be able to develop meaningful friendships with white students. Was he prepared academically to handle a white college? What would it be like living away from home? Could Rev. Bailey be right?

The sign on the highway read, "Welcome to Danville." Reggie felt excited but a bit nervous. Suddenly it occurred to him he was about to enter new territory where he didn't know a soul. As the bus snaked through the streets towards the station, he noticed that the town seemed quieter than Smoky Mountain. There weren't as many stores or as many people on the streets. The bus rolled up to the station that was in what must have been the center of town. Across from the station was a café with no signs of life except the blinking neon sign. Two blocks north, Reggie could see a sign for Rexall Drugs and to the south was a Kresses Five and Dime store, both familiar sights. Two blocks east of the station was a street that was probably the main street. There were city buses picking up and discharging passengers. Reggie collected his belongings and walked through the station to the opposite side and onto the street where he found a few taxis lined up. A driver asked, "You need a taxi, young man?"

"Yes sir," Reggie quickly answered, wondering how much this ride would set him back. The driver was a Negro whose dry skin made him look like he was in his seventies. He asked Reggie where he was going and where he was from. Reggie answered and the driver went silent for the remainder of the trip.

The ride to Davis took Reggie through a neighborhood with stately homes and spacious lawns that reminded him of the neighborhood surrounding the country club in Smoky Mountain where he once worked. As the taxi drove onto the campus, he noticed the ivy laced buildings, the spacious green grass campus, the Gothic architecture interwoven with modern designs and students milling around. "One day," Reggie thought, "they will call me a Davis man."

"This is where you wanted to go ain't it?" The driver asked as the car stopped in front of the dormitory.

"Yes, sir," Reggie said.

"Well here it is." There was a note of disgust in his voice.

Somebody else must have made the driver mad and he hasn't gotten over it, Reggie decided. Reggie looked up at this light grey stone brick building with tall, polished wooden doors. He smiled. It looked like a mansion. The doors swung open and a couple of students fanned out. Reggie stepped in before they closed and was greeted by a friendly student who seemed to be in charge. Before he could ask a question, the friendly student said, "Good afternoon, Mr. Morton. My name is Jeff Anderson and I'm the dorm counselor. Welcome to Davis. I hope you had a pleasant trip." The friendly greeting from this baby-faced guy with dark red hair helped Reggie begin to relax. He smiled and reached to shake the counselor's hand.

"How do you do Mr. Anderson? I had a nice trip."

"Very good, I will help you get settled. First, why don't you go over to the desk and let them know you have arrived. They have a package for you with all the instructions you will need for the next few days, including your room assignment. If you have questions, I am here."

Reggie thanked him and walked to the reception desk, which was crowded with large brown envelopes and a pile of numbered keys. A jolly boy wearing a name tag that read Fred Lewis reached for Reggie's hand and said, "This is where it all begins," then patiently explained what was in his package and invited Reggie to return for any questions he might have.

Reggie's room was on the third floor with a view of the Southern end of the campus where he could see faculty housing. Below his window was a parking lot for dorm residents. The room was sparsely furnished with two of everything, but it was clean. The mattress on the bed was thinner than the one he slept on at home but it was comfortable enough. Reggie couldn't believe he had his own desk. He immediately claimed the space next to the window before his roommate arrived.

By the time he was settled-in, his stomach began to growl. Foregoing the brown bag his mother had prepared, he decided to check out what was being served at the student union. He entered this spacious dining room with booths lined against one wall and tables for four scattered throughout. On the side opposite the booths was the cafeteria-style serving station. A line of students were passing through, choosing dishes and chatting. Very few tables had been occupied. Reggie marched to the long line and selected his food. He noticed none of the servers were Negro which surprised him and made him a bit nervous.

By the time he was ready to find a seat, nearly half of the tables had been taken. He spotted one near the entrance and sat down. There was not another Negro face in the whole place. At one time or the other, just about everyone in the cafeteria stared in his direction with what looked like stern curiosity, but nobody greeted him. He felt scared and began to consume the hamburger faster than he would have at Harlem House while thinking that maybe he should have stayed in his room and cleaned out that brown bag his mother had prepared. As soon as the last French fry was entering his mouth, he pushed back his seat, deposited his tray and tried to walk out at a normal pace, though he could feel himself quickening. When he got outside, he wanted to run, but figured that if someone saw him, they might think that he was a stranger than usual Negro.

As he walked back to his room without losing any time, it suddenly occurred to him that his roommate was probably white. What if he dislikes Negroes? The possibility was so disturbing that Reggie dismissed it. He opened the door and found the room was the same as he left it. The roommate would probably arrive later that night or the next day, he concluded.

It had been a long day and he was feeling exhausted so he lay on the bed to relax for a few minutes before his roommate probably arrived. When he awoke it was very quiet. He looked at the clock on his desk. It was a half-hour past midnight.

He was wide awake now and the events of the day began to play back in his mind. Why had the taxi driver reacted the way he did? Had someone killed one of the Negroes that enrolled here last year? He felt his face flush. It dawned on him that Jeff called his name before he told him. How did he know who he was? Did he know all the students in the dorm by name? Surely, there was at least one other Negro living in the dorm? Come to think of it, he couldn't recall seeing any Negroes yet. Take it easy Reggie, take it easy, you have only been here a matter of hours, he told himself.

Reggie was awakened the next morning by the sound of foot steps and chatter in the hall. After collecting his thoughts and realizing where he was, he searched for the schedule of activities for the day. There was nothing scheduled for the morning. At 1:00 P.M. there were Greek House receptions. He had received an invitation from Omega Alpha about two weeks before arriving on campus. He was very impressed and had looked forward to going, but was having reservations after last night, but it was too early to start dodging things. After all, they did send him an invitation. There was the freshman dance at eight. Maybe by that time a friendly roommate would have arrived.

He hauled himself out of bed, grabbed his robe and headed for the shower. A very pale boy was wrapped in a white towel shaving. Reggie said good morning and the boy turned towards him with a look of shock and said, "Good morning."

Reggie stepped into the shower. He relaxed under the pulsating motion of the water over his body. He grew up taking baths and he wasn't used to showers. It felt so good that he lingered for a while. Once he could focus through the steam he heard whispers, but could not discern what was being said. He then began to notice every few seconds someone would walk past the shower and turn their head in his direction. It happened so many times he was sure it was deliberate.

After finishing his shower, he leaped into his robe and marched straight to his room. He noticed that the shower room was full of students just milling around. Back in his room, Reggie began to feel angry. He was no freak show there for the amusement of white students. He didn't want to go to breakfast where he was sure the show would go on. However, his hunger was more powerful than his pride. As he was about to cross the street on his way to the student union, a car passed driven by a white woman with a Negro sitting next to her in the front seat and a white girl in the back. Another Negro, thank God. He watched the car, hoping it would stop and he could see who got out and how they interacted, but the car turned the corner out of sight. As he approached the door to the student union, a girl in front of him stumbled and dropped some books. Reggie picked them up and handed them to her. She smiled and said, "How clumsy of me. Thanks for your help."

Reggie felt a moment of joy; someone had acknowledged him and said a kind word. It didn't matter that it was no more than thanks and a smile. He walked into the student union feeling a slight rise in confidence. The roving eyes continued through his meal and he avoided them by looking at his plate. He walked back to the dormitory expecting to find his roommate.

Unconsciously, he began to whistle the tune, "What a friend we have in Jesus," a song he learned in Sunday school. When he realized what he was doing, a smile crept through his lips. Maybe I am receiving a message from on high, he pondered.

His return to an empty room wiped the smile off his face. Maybe his roommate was an upper classman and they were not due on campus for two more days.

Reggie remembered the reception at Omega Alpha and felt unsure. Maybe if Jeff figured out who he was before he arrived, there was a good chance Omega Alpha did too. Well, at least I have to give it a try, he decided. He began pulling out those tailor made pants and coordinated shirts, trying to decide which would make the best impression. The navy blue pants and the white-striped shirt won. He took one last look in the mirror and turned left and right while adjusting his belt, then strolled out and headed towards Greek Row, feeling the effects of anxiety bubbling in his legs.

Greek Row was a very clean street with no debris anywhere, lined with manicured lawns and mansions bearing Greek lettering on their facades. Reggie was awed but still nervous. He turned from the street and started up the walkway to the house with the Omega Alpha sign. It was a two-story red brick building with tall white columns adorning the entrance at the end of a concrete walkway. Reggie took only a few steps up the walkway when a tall, slim, white guy in blue jeans and a Davis sweatshirt, with a look of disgust plastered on his face, rushed out to meet him.

"We don't pledge Negroes," he blurted out without any kind of greeting. "If you received an invitation to the reception it was a mistake, sorry." He turned around and walked back into the house.

Reggie felt like he was worth less than a penny. He didn't know what to do or say. He stood frozen in his tracks for a moment under the roving eyes of some students watching the incident from their windows. Finally he felt secure enough to walk without stumbling. He lifted his head and looked straight forward trying to disguise his humiliation. Anger swelled in him. Who do these no-color, poor-hygiene peckerwoods think they are? They are no better than the crooked cops in Smoky Mountain. Maybe Alfred was right: there would be no welcoming mat into white heaven.

The day was bright and sunny. Reggie decided to walk around and cool-down instead of returning to his room. As he explored the walkways, he found himself in a beautiful garden around a pond separated from the main campus by a wooded path. The lingering blossoms from summer flowers stood in strategic locations. The scene was tranquil. All he could hear was the sound of hissing bugs, singing birds and splashing water.

Reggie took a seat on one of the benches spread over the garden. He closed his eyes, rested his head on the trunk of a tree behind the bench and gave in to the tears that were tugging to be released. Nobody was around so he let them flow freely. After a few moments, he opened his eyes. The sun overhead was almost blinding. "Dear God", he prayed. "Please help me cope." At that moment the face of his mother entered his mind. His heart beat slowed and the anger seemed to dissipate. What if things get worse and I can't study. Returning home after flunking out would be horrible, he pondered. That will not happen he vowed.

As Reggie started up the steps to the dorm, Jeff was coming out. He greeted Reggie and asked how he was doing. Reggie was not about to spill his guts to Jeff, so he choked it back and said that he was doing just fine. He asked Jeff when his roommate was due to arrive.

Jeff looked up with a nervous smile and said, "Mr. Morton or may I call you Reginald?"

"Call me Reggie."

"Well Reggie you are one of the lucky students on campus. You do not have a roommate. You have your room all to yourself. How about that, a freshman with his own room. The student we assigned to be your roommate decided at the last minute not to come to Davis. So you became a lucky freshman."

Reggie felt like another hammer had hit him in the stomach. He knew Jeff was lying. It was written all over his face. Reggie thanked him and headed to his room. Maybe it wasn't all bad. It might be good to hide in his own room while recovering from the many insults that he anticipated facing. What if the guy was as prejudiced as those at Omega Alpha? Maybe this is the answer to another one of Mother's prayers.

Reggie remembered the freshman dance and wondered if he could stomach any more humiliation that day. The dance could be a real embarrasssment. "The hell with it all," he shouted in his room. "I can take it and make it without being a martyr" He laid back on the bed thinking what to write to Mona. He wanted to tell someone about what was happening to him, but that kind of news might worry her. She seemed to be having the opposite experience and he didn't want to spoil that. He drifted off to sleep. When he awoke he felt rested and energized. He decided he was not going to hide in his room. He would go out and face the enemy.

As Reggie left the dorm and started to walk towards the gym where the dance was being held, a group of students began whispering and laughing behind him. They appeared to deliberately stay behind. It made him angry. He was sure they were talking about him. *They can kiss me where the good Lord split me and if one of them tries something they are going to get everything I have upside their lily white heads*, he said to himself. He tried to maintain a normal pace to camouflage his fear. As he approached the entrance to the gym, the group rushed forward and surrounded him. There were six white girls all smiling. He recognized one. She was the girl who slipped on the steps to the student union and dropped her books and smiled at him when he picked them up. She looked at him and said, "Let's go dance."

Reggie felt weak in the knees, but he commanded his legs not to give out on him now. Sweat appeared on his forehead, but he was too embarrassed to wipe it. Excitement swept through him like an electric charge. He entered the gym like a king surrounded by the court's ladies- in- waiting. The music greeted them and they fell into a group of square dancers. Country music and square dancing was not Reggie's idea of having a good time, but he was glad to be with friendly faces and he wasn't about to complain. He stepped in rhythm with the music although he had never square danced before. He felt silly. What would his friends back home think if they could see him now? When it finally ended, the group of girls seemed exhausted and decided they needed something to drink. They asked Reggie to join them as they headed for the refreshment stand. He fell in the long line of thirsty dancers immediately behind the girls.

Another group of girls came over and began to chat with the six girls accompanying Reggie. They inched their way into the line, pushing Reggie further back. He looked out at the crowd and found many eyes on the girls and him. He didn't know whether to be proud or scared. He quickly turned his eyes towards the refreshment table. He didn't want to express any discomfort that might turn off the girls. They got their drinks and stood waiting for him. While Reggie was collecting his drink, the music started again. As he approached the girls a group of white boys rushed over and took the hands of each of the girls and pulled them to the dance floor. Reggie was left standing alone, one hand holding his drink and the other in his pocket.

As he stood there surveying the place and wondering what to do, a group of dancers swayed to their left, leaving a view of the other end of the gym. Reggie was startled to see three Negroes, one boy and two girls. He felt like running over and hugging them. They were looking in his direction, but when they realized he had seen them, they quickly turned their heads, pretending they hadn't noticed him. That slowed Reggie down a bit, but he was not about to let that deter him. He didn't know what to do about the six girls that escorted him in the dance. However, he figured those boys that dragged them onto the dance floor were making a statement and he was relieved to let them make it.

His heart pumping in high gear, Reggie strolled over to the Negro students and introduced himself. The boy extended his hand, and said, "I am Ron. This is Sandra, and Nancy." With an artificial smile and her nose slightly upturned, Sandra asked, "Where are you from?"

"Smoky Mountain. I live in the dorm. I arrived yesterday. Where are you from?"

"We live in Danville," Sandra answered.

"How did you end up in Davis?" Sandra asked, looking like a fly had just landed on her face.

"I have a scholarship. What are you majoring in?" Reggie asked.

"Elementary Education."

"What about you Ron?" Reggie asked.

"Well, I'm working this year and if I am not drafted into the Army, I plan to go to Tennessee State next year."

Reggie was thankful that Ron was there. He thought the girls were acting like he was wearing bad deodorant.

Sandra let out a belly laugh and said, "Can you believe that?" She pointed to a black/white couple dancing unrestrained around the floor. Reggie was surprised. He recognized them both. It was the Negro he saw in the car with the white family driving onto the campus when he was heading for breakfast. The girl was the one in the back seat. It looked like they both were students and it appeared they were a couple that didn't give a damn about the roomful of stares they were receiving. They danced like no one else was around. Reggie asked who they were. Nancy looked as if she just remembered he was around. She said, "We don't know." She looked at Sandra and Ron as if they were an exclusive group that didn't trust Reggie.

The music became more amenable to jitterbugging and the four paired off and began to dance, Reggie and Nancy, Roy and Sandra. As the evening went on, and the music permitted, they continued to dance, but they were not focused on each other. Like everybody else, their eyes continued to follow the mixed couple.

After the band played its last song, Reggie said good night and he looked forward to seeing them all again and that he would look out for Nancy and Sandra on campus. He was feeling better than he had since arriving. As he walked to the dorm, he began to think about everything that happened to him that day. Could Negroes and whites get along despite the history of segregation or were the students at Omega Alpha the norm? How was he supposed to react to the prejudiced whites he interacted with daily?

Maybe he was overreacting, he though. With exulting noise coming from the hall, Reggie sat in the security of his room and wrote to Mona about the freshman dance; the Negroes he met; and how he square danced for the first time.

8

Reggie slept well that night after the Freshmen dance and was awakened by the bright sun shining through his window. There was no noise in the hallway so he dashed to the shower which he assumed to be empty. It was. He showered quickly, returned to his room and reached for the registration instructions. They seemed complicated and massive, but he felt confident he understood what needed to be done; he just hoped he could make it through the day without any humiliating experiences.

Registration took place in the gym, but it had been transformed from the dance hall of the night before. There were a series of stalls lined up against the wall with a professor behind each one. Students waited in a line, shifting their weight from leg to leg, clasping the registration forms in their hands, looking at their watches and anxiously hoping that the class they wanted would stay open. Reggie figured that the longest lines must be for required courses. The annoyed professors did not pay any special attention to Reggie when he reached the front of their lines. However, there were the occasional whispers from students when they saw him. Reggie saw two other Negroes registering on the opposite side of the gym; but they had disappeared when he finished. He wondered where Sandra and Nancy were. Maybe they were still taking the placement tests. He ended up with all the classes he wanted, but had no idea who the professors were.

He took a detour on his way back to the dorm and went to the book store to begin purchasing supplies. While he was scanning the book shelves, someone walked up behind him and whispered,

"You deserted us last night." Reggie's face flushed. He turned around with a nervous smile and there was the girl he had come to know as the one whose books he picked up one day.

He swallowed and said, "I didn't mean to desert you. You all seemed to be very busy. I enjoyed our dance. I think I am a better square dancer after last night, thanks to you. By the way, my name is Reggie Morton."

"I'm Betty Duvall and it is my pleasure to meet you Reggie Morton. Where are you from?" Reggie explained he was from Smoky Mountain, Tennessee. And Betty proudly announced she was from Nashville. She looked at her watch and said,

"I have to go, but I will see you around."

"Yes, OK," Reggie said with a stroke of euphoria charging through his body. He couldn't help but notice how Betty's long blond hair trailed down her back and how her body resembled Mona's. Her eyes were sky blue and she had a small narrow nose that gave her a sophisticated look. She gave the appearance of being delicate and vulnerable, the kind of person you would want to protect. But she also had an air of mischief. Reggie laughed at himself for immediately thinking of taking a bite of "forbidden fruit" just because someone was nice to him. What would Mona think if she could read his thoughts now? Realizing that he was laughing for the first time in a couple of days, he strolled to his dorm.

As Reggie was passing through the dorm's lobby that evening on his way to dinner, he noticed the back of a Negro who had just exited the building and was walking down the steps. He began to increase his pace in order to catch up. He immediately realized that it was the guy who danced the night away with the white girl.

"Hey there, can I borrow your dance shoes?" Reggie called out.

The guy turned to see where the voice was coming from and immediately responded, "Any time you think your feet can fit into them." They both laughed. "I'm Robert Butler."

"I'm Reggie Morton. Where are you headed?"

"To dinner, how about you?

"Me too, how about me joining you?"

"Let's go."

During dinner Robert said he was from Olive Branch, about sixty miles east of Danville. He lived in the same dorm as Reggie, on the fourth floor, and also had no roommate. Reggie thought maybe the administration didn't realize that Robert was Negro since they could have put them together. Maybe they wanted to do their best to isolate them and add to their frustration. Reggie asked who the chick was that Robert was dancing with last night. Robert explained she was the daughter of the woman his mother worked for and they had known each other for a couple of years. He told Reggie he applied to Davis without telling his mother or anyone else. He knew Davis was the school of choice for whites in Tennessee and the Brown decision made it possible for him to go there. He swore that he had no idea Julia was planning to go there as well. When he got accepted he spilled the news all over town. His mother was surprised and proud. Julia was ecstatic and told him she was looking forward to getting "closer."

Robert was aware that Julia's mother was wary of her daughter's curiosity about Negroes. Once, when she was eight, she wandered into a revival service at the Negro Baptist Church. When her mother finally found her, Julia was clapping, throwing her hands in the air and twisting her body. Her social activities were restricted for a month after that incident and she was told socializing with Negroes was absolutely forbidden. However, Robert believed Julia's mother had grown to trust him and considered the relationship between him and her daughter as harmless, especially after she offered to drive them both to Davis and asked him to look after her.

"I don't know what Julia means by 'closer' relationship but I'm hoping it means I can get 'some' every now and then. Not so sure about being seen around with a white girl after seeing what happened to Emmett Till, but I made a promise to look after her.

It seems like you are a big hit already, walking into the dance with six fine white chicks on your arm," Robert said.

"That was what I would call an answer to one of those prayers my mother sent up to heaven. Those girls surrounded me and asked me to dance. What kind of fool would I be to say no."

"Well, the details are not what people saw, so I am afraid you might have to live with that reputation for a while," Robert said. "If last night is any indication, there may be lean pickings on campus with regards to dating Negro chicks. We will probably have to go into town to find us a fine Sapphire. Who were those bats you ended up with? One looked like she was having a love affair with sweets and was allergic to make-up."

"That had to be Nancy." Reggie answered.

"The other one looked like she had risen up out of the grave."

"Well, the only one left is Sandra," Reggie said. They both laughed. Reggie defended the girls by saying they were a little icy but would probably warm up with a few compliments. Robert just needed to get to know them. Reggie made it clear he wasn't worried about dating because he had the girl he would always love.

Robert laughed and said, "Yeah, yeah."

"No kidding, she is fine as wine in the summertime and crazy about me. She cried when she found out we were not going to the same college, but she writes me all the time. I'm set." Reggie insisted.

"Hey, whatever you say," Robert said with his hands lifted in the air as if he was being searched by police.

After dinner Robert and Reggie started back across campus towards the dorm. Robert excused himself. He had to meet Julia. Reggie strolled back to his room bounding in his steps. He sat down and wrote another letter to Mona telling her how happy he was that he had met another Negro living in the dorm and described him as friendly, with a sense of humor, but who was sometimes overconfident and loud, which might be a reaction to his unfortunate looks. He had large lips, a broad nose, a small shaped head and some misdirected teeth. But the good Lord had seen fit to give him an athletic body with wide shoulders.

"Yes, Rev. Bailey, I have what it takes," Reggie said as he turned off the lights. Tomorrow would be his first day of classes with white students.

9

Davis was the premier university in the state. It dated back to the early 1800s at the beginning of the land grant college movement where the states allocated land for the building of higher educational institutions. At the entrance to the campus was a large granite stone engraved with the names of students that died in the Civil War. The Who's-Who of the state's white community was among their alumni. After the Brown decision, it was rumored that Dr. Peter Roberts, the school's president, had said it was probably time for him to move on because he didn't see himself supporting that decision. The state had provided for Negroes in their own schools so why would the government want to interfere with something that worked. The school successfully fought the order to integrate in 1955, 56 and 57, but lost the battle in 1958. The school had had its fill of Rev. Alton Williams and his Civil Rights organization when they finished with them at the end of the school year in 1957. They had been defeated in all their delay tactics but refused to let go of their anger. There was no other place to direct it except on the innocent Negro students who had the audacity to enroll. They felt good about the first year of integration because out of the seven that enrolled, only three returned for the second year and there had been no outrage from the Negro community. This year only four had enrolled and the faculty wondered how many would be there this time next year. Reggie's application had been widely discussed. He had all the credentials for the financial aid package he received, but they did not want to give it to him. The determining factor pushing them to award it was, no one, absolutely no one, wanted any further contact with Rev. Williams. They weren't sure whether he was behind Reggie's application and they didn't want to take a chance.

These had been trying times for Dr. Roberts. The governor had convinced him to stay on while they fought the battle to circumvent the court order. Now that that fight was lost, he didn't want it to seem like he had been forced out, but staying on made him feel like he was eating crow. He was a native of Kentucky, but kept a small Confederate flag on the bookshelf in his office. Most of the faculty was Southerners. There were a few who were immigrants from Europe and some from the northern states. A small percentage of them even thought integration was a good thing for educational institutions.

10

Reggie's first class was Freshman English. The instructor was called Dr. Mark Schulman and he had a heavy white Southern accent. He looked like he was in his fifties or early sixties, with a receding hair line and a protruding stomach. His speech and body language spoke loudly that he was a no-nonsense sort of professor. As he outlined the course and his expectations, Reggie took copious notes. He was the only Negro in the class. There were stares coming at him from all directions. It felt like a jury was trying to decide whether to throw him into a pot of boiling hot oil, hang him from a tree or chop him up limb by limb. At the end of his summary, Dr. Schulman announced he had an assignment. He was going to write a topic sentence on the black board and each student was to develop it in the remaining thirty minutes of the class. With his short arm and fleshy hand, he wrote, "College gives me the opportunity to...."

When the bell rang Reggie felt good about what he had written. Prof. Schulman stood near the door to collect the papers as the class exited. Reggie smiled as he handed him his work, but Dr. Schulman did not reciprocate. As a matter of fact he seemed to have frowned. Reggie tried to dismiss that assumption. He had to admit he really didn't notice Dr. Schulman's reactions to anyone else.

Reggie's second class was math. Professor Dawson James looked to be somewhere in his middle sixties, neatly dressed with an accent that obviously wasn't Southern. He spoke too fast for a Southerner, Reggie decided. He moved around in short, deliberate steps, always in perfect posture like someone who had been trained in the military. He seemed so devoted to his subject matter that he did not seem to notice any particular student. His demeanor and the tone of his voice didn't change and the 50 minute class flew by.

Two down and four to go. Maybe things won't be that bad, Reggie thought. No one tried to spit on me or openly call me a Nigger. Just before approaching the lecture hall for Sociology he felt a weight on the heels of his shoes. The hall wasn't that crowded so there was no need for someone to cluster that close to him. When he turned around,two white boys stared at him with menacing looks, daring him to say something. He continued to class without a word. He was so shocked he couldn't think of what would have been an appropriate reaction. It was so much more aggressive than any of the reactions he had experienced so far. He tried to disguise his feelings by looking at the numbers on the doors of the rooms lining the hall.

As he sat down trying to coach his heart back into its normal pace, Professor Alvin Woodcliff entered the room with great energy and confidence. He was short in stature, had closely cropped hair and a sad, mean face resembling pictures of Napoleon.

He wasted no time. As soon as he laid down his books and papers he turned to the blackboard and wrote his name; then he turned around and began to outline the course and give his reading list. He spoke with the drawl of a born and bred white Southerner. Once he had completed the preliminaries, he slowed his pace of speech and said to the class.

"You know Davis has fought hard to keep Negroes out of the school, but that battle seems to have been lost. I guess that is something we will have to get used to the same as we get used to paying taxes. Since they are here maybe we will have a chance to study first hand the validity of perceived notions about them."

He never looked in Reggie's direction. Some of the students shifted in their seats; while others whispered to each other and smiled while turning their heads toward Reggie. If Reggie were white, he would have looked like a ghost. His hands and feet shook as he tried to hide his hurt. When class was over, he immediately rose from his seat and wobbled a little before regaining his composure. He was glad that he had a break before his next class. He needed to withdraw and find a way to regroup. He had no appetite now and decided to escape to his room where he could be completely alone.

As soon as his door closed, images of the boy at Omega Alpha, the bruises on Doug's face after the police beating and the mutilated body of Emmett Till flashed before him. What am I doing here? I could be at Lane College or maybe Howard University. I don't have to put up with this, he declared. He dropped down on the bed and landed on a letter from Mona he had forgotten all about. He placed it over his heart and visualized holding Mona close before opening it.

Her letter talked about being surrounded by students who had gone to exclusive private schools and seemed to be better prepared for college than she was. However, she claimed she was gaining more confidence each day she sat in class alongside of them. She talked about the different students she had gotten to know and how she was learning how to get around New York. She didn't mention any male students at Columbia University. Reggie missed her terribly. He felt being near her was what he needed to bring back some joy to his life. He wondered what he could tell her when answering the letter. He put it down, stretched out on the bed and closed his eyes dreading his next class, American History.

When Reggie walked into the lecture hall, Dr. Elizabeth Thorn was at the podium looking over her black rimed glasses attached to a chain dangling around her neck. It seemed she was trying to size up each student. When she saw Reggie, she smiled and said, "Good afternoon." Reggie felt like he had suddenly lost ten pounds. His steps were lighter as he moved to a seat. Blood seemed to travel to parts of his body other than his head. He thanked god under his breath as he slumped down in the seat. The lecture went by quickly and Reggie only remembered small pieces.

Dr. Thorn pulled him aside after class and asked him where he was from and how he had chosen Davis. He proudly answered that he was on scholarship. She wished him the best for success in his studies. Reggie strolled down the hall thinking he should write home and tell his mother he knew she was praying for him and God had answered her prayers. In the midst of Hell, he had found an angel.

Reggie was writing to Mona about Dr. Thorn when he heard a heavy knock on the door. It was so loud it frightened him. He wondered what he was in for now. When he opened it, there was Robert looking distressed.

"Hey, what's happening? Did someone threaten you? Come in." Reggie said.

"I can't find Julia," Robert blurted out. "I've looked all over and when I call the dorm they just say she is not here at the moment. I asked a couple of girls she knows if they had seen her. Nobody saw her leave the dorm or the campus. I waited outside her European History class, but she never came out and nobody said they saw her. When I was walking back to her dorm, some girl ran over to me and said Julia was called to the Dean's office before her first class and she hadn't been seen since. I don't know what to do. I wonder if there was an emergency that sent her home. I don't want to get her parents upset by calling. Her mother told me to look after her."

Reggie told him to sit down and take it easy. He suggested they walk back over to Julia's dorm and see if she had turned up. Robert immediately agreed. Students outside her dorm began to whisper when they saw the two of them coming. The girl at the desk said she was not there. When they were leaving, a girl yelled, "Did you lose your honey?"

Robert remained in Reggie's room until around midnight going over his story again and again as if the answer to the riddle would pop up. Reggie tried to assure him that if it was something really serious the school would have intervened and taken care of it. Robert agreed, probably because he was too tired to disagree. But Reggie wasn't convinced by his own words.

The next day when Reggie was leaving his physical education class one of the other students was exiting the locker room at the same time.

"I'm Harry Dubinski."

Reggie was surprised and immediately extended his hand. "I'm Reggie Morton."

"Where are you from?" Harry asked.

"Smoky Mountain, Tennessee and you?"

"Chicago, the Windy city."

"What are you doing in Tennessee?"

"Davis School of Pharmacy. What brings you here?" Harry inquired. Reggie explained his scholarship. Could this be another friendly person or another spectator for the freak show? Reggie wondered. They both lived in the dorm, Harry on the fifth floor and Reggie the third. Harry seemed nervous, but Reggie thought it was probably because it had been hard for Harry to approach him.

As they were about to reach Richter Hall where classes were held, Harry realized there was little time left for asking the question that was pressing his mind. He wasn't sure how to approach it. He didn't want to say something insulting and ruin this opportunity to develop a friendship with a Negro.

He had counted on more of them on campus considering segregation in schools had been declared unconstitutional. There was just a hand full of Negroes in his high school, but he had never been close to any. His family never said bad things about Negroes, but there were never any around. His family's servants were Mexican. He took a deep breath and with his voice shaking said, "Reggie, is that your girlfriend they sent home yesterday?"

Reggie snapped, "No, my girlfriend goes to Barnard College in New York City. What girl are you talking about? Who sent her home and why did they send her home?" As soon as the last syllable escaped his lips, Reggie knew who the girl was.

Harry's body tensed. "I heard the girl was sent home before her first class. They said she was unsuited for Davis."

"What does 'unsuited' for Davis mean?" Reggie asked.

"I just heard the rumor in the dorm last night." Harry said with a slight stutter. "I have to get to class. I'm in room 511. Let's get together some time." Harry said as he trotted away.

Reggie couldn't figure out why Julia was forced out and not Robert. That's the opposite of how it usually happens. Maybe Julia rejected their demand that she stop seeing Robert. Reggie didn't remember much about the Psychology class except Dr. Barbara Caton paced up and down the aisles and seemed young for a professor. During the entire fifty minutes, his mind was stuck on whether Robert already knew what had happened, or how he would take the news if he didn't and wondering what kind of place Davis really was. The sound of the bell ending class startled him. He wondered what he had missed or if there was an assignment. He ambled out of class trying hard not to reveal his thoughts to the sea of white students surrounding him. His walk to the dorm was slow as he tried to calculate what had happened. He knew he would soon face Robert and he hadn't come-up with a plan to deal with him. He felt that he was as angry as Robert would be. Time to develop a plan immediately expired. Robert was approaching.

"Something is seriously wrong. Julia still hasn't shown up." Robert said. He looked tired and his eyes were red as if he had not slept for days. Reggie's mind went spinning for the right thing to say. His mouth opened and he said, "Come on let's go up to my room."

Reggie walked ahead while Robert continued to say, "God damn! God damn! What's going on here?" Once they were in the room, Robert began to pace the floor. Reggie put his hand on Robert's shoulder and said, "You've got to pull yourself together. Julia has been sent home." Robert froze.

"What do you mean, sent home, who sent her home? Was she hurt?" Reggie explained what he had heard and why he thought it had happened. Robert sat with his face in his hands, shaking his head. "I wondered if I had anything to do with it. I hoped and prayed I didn't. I thought they would come after me, not her. They always blame us for everything. Her mother will blame me.

They can't be letting me off the hook. They must have a plan for punishing me too. What have I gotten myself into and what have I done to Julia? What the hell am I going to do now?"

"Calm down, calm down." Reggie tried to focus him. "First, you don't need to worry about Julia's future. She will do just fine after getting over the shock of what happened. Her pride has been wounded but in time she will heal. Her parents will send her to another school. She has options."

"But what about how she feels about me? Her mother's not going to let her see me again," Robert protested.

Obviously, Julia's affections had meant more to Robert than he had let on. "Buddy, you and Julia will have many more lovers in your life." Reggie said and then cringed at the thought that it could apply to him and Mona. "Now come on and do what Negroes have done all our lives: double our determination and move on. Let's start by getting some grub."

11

SUNDAY NIGHT CAME MUCH TOO FAST FOR REGGIE. HE WASN'T READY TO face Monday morning. There had not been enough time to heal from the first week. Thoughts of what he may be in for on Monday made him feel nauseous. He wanted to believe things would get better; but what if integration only meant you had to stand side by side with daily in your face discrimination and rejection because of the color of his skin and find a way to succeed in spite of it , he wondered.

As he drifted off to sleep, he began dreaming. He saw himself trying to escape a group of white students with painted faces chasing him towards another group of cheering students. They were closing in on him from both directions. He fell down and one of them drew a pistol and pointed it at him. He woke up in a cold sweat. The dream was so disturbing he couldn't go back to sleep. He tossed and turned the rest of the night. I wish I could hold Mona close and hear her say she loves me. I wish Davis would burn down so I could return home without letting people know what it really is like here, he fantasized.

When dawn finally arrived Reggie was tired and wanted to stay in his room, but didn't want to explain his absence to anyone who might notice.

"Wait up," a voice called from behind as Reggie slowly walked to English Composition.

"Where were you this week-end? I knocked on your door a couple of times but no one answered." Harry asked.

"I was around. You must have come by during the few times I stepped out of the room."

"I'll check you out this evening after classes. Maybe, I'll give you a chance to beat me at a game of chess," Harry said with a smile.

"I don't know about that, but I'll bring along my checker board and see how good you are," Reggie winked.

Reggie didn't know exactly what to make of Harry. He seemed more relaxed and friendly than the last time when he dashed away like he had seen a ghost. Maybe this guy could be a friend and Lord knows I need as many friends as I can get. Robert was the only person he had been able to talk with since the freshman dance and he was still wrestling with the loss of Julia. Reggie also felt himself becoming more and more uncomfortable with Robert. He was loud and boisterous and such behavior would embarrass Reggie when it could be observed by white people.

Reggie said goodbye to Harry and walked in early for class. As he entered the room he noticed Dr. Schulman was already there sitting at his desk. "Good morning, Sir," Reggie said, in keeping with his Southern home training. When Dr. Schulman looked up and saw Reggie, he went back to reading without saying a word. Reggie's first response was surprise and then anger. He wanted to walk out and wait until the other students arrived but quickly discarded that thought. It would be too obvious a defeat and would probably indicate to Dr. Schulman that he was easily intimidated. Reggie sat in anger as the classroom filled and the lecture began. Dr. Schulman's first order of business was to return the essays done at the first class. The students to Reggie's left and right received their papers before him. Both had a sea of red marks on them, but with a big 'C' at the top of the page. When Reggie received his there were a total of three red marks, but at the top was a 'C—' His mouth went dry and his hands began to shake. He couldn't understand the difference between his grade and the white students' grades. This prejudiced bastard could flunk me no matter how hard I try, Reggie quickly concluded. If he thinks he's going to stop me, he's got another thought coming, Reggie vowed.

PART III – A DAVIS MAN

12

After Dr. Schulman's class, Reggie wanted to curse or kick anyone looking at him with a disapproving eye. He bit his bottom lip, balled up his fist and pounded his thigh. "All I'm trying to do is get a good education and a decent job," he thought, "and this prejudiced peckerwood won't defeat me. The law of the land says I ought to be able to get that education here." He started towards his next class with his back straight and taking deliberate steps as if he had been ordered by a sergeant to march into battle. Professor James and Dr. Caton continued to conduct class as if his presence was nothing unusual. There also appeared to be less stares in those classes.

His physical education teacher, Mr. Cosman Alexander, spoke in a commanding voice with an accent Reggie did not recognize. He referred to all the students as mister and seldom ever smiled at anyone. At the end of that class, Reggie felt relieved but beaten and wanted to crawl under the covers of his bed and forget the world for a while.

He charged towards his room as fast as he could without running or bringing attention to himself. As soon as the door closed behind him he fell on the bed fully clothed. He was awakened by a knock on the door and a voice whispering, "Reggie, Reggie." He sat up trying to pull himself out of sleep and wandered to the door without time to think who it was. There stood Harry with a forced, curious smile on his face and a chess set under his arm.

"I thought I missed you again. I knocked about seven times with no answer."

"I was sleep," Reggie said. He looked at the clock on his desk and realized he had been asleep for hours.

"So are you ready to lose a chess game?"

"Right now, I could eat a horse. How about let's have dinner first."

"I guess you need your energy to take me on. I can handle dinner," Harry smiled. That response threw Reggie into a full awaken state. He's not embarrassed to be seen with me in the student union. I guess he can't be all that bad, Reggie decided.

During dinner Harry kept his eyes on their table without casting them at the other students. Reggie couldn't figure what that meant, but he noticed there weren't as many stares as when he ate alone or with Robert.

After dinner they returned to Reggie's room. Reggie didn't know a thing about chess, but he decided to let Harry teach him since he seemed so excited about the game. Harry had never thought of teaching someone to play. He grew up around the game and learned by watching. He laid the board out on the floor, rolled out the parts and began rattling off their names, pawns, bishops, kings, isolated pawns, backward pawns, paused pawns, and rooks. He then hesitated as if he was looking for the next step. Reggie detected his discomfort which made him a bit uncomfortable. He decided to throw Harry a rope and hopefully relieve both of their tensions.

"When did you become interested in the game?" Reggie asked.

Harry took up the rope with a glisten in his eyes. "My father loved the game and I used to watch him play with anyone who stopped by. When I was around eight he invited me to sit for a game. We were both surprised how much I knew. He said, 'That's my boy.' That's the only time I can remember he really seemed proud of me. We were not close and he didn't seem to mind. He died of cancer when I was sixteen. My mom remarried two years ago and I am still getting used to my stepfather."

Reggie was curious, but didn't know if he should probe further about the stepfather Harry was trying to get used to; however, he knew it was up to him to keep the conversation going since Harry had paused.

"Do you know how to play checkers?" Reggie asked.

With what seemed like a condescending smile, Harry said, "No, I never have played checkers."

"Well, one day I might teach you."

This guy really seems okay, Reggie kept thinking, but he couldn't help wondering about this white boy who came from the north to a school in the South. Weren't there any good pharmacy schools in the north? Reggie wondered.Harry looked up at the clock and realized it was eleven and he had an eight o'clock class. He nervously announced that he had lost track of time and stood up quickly from the floor and knocked over a bottle of ink that was on the edge of Reggie's desk. The ink spilled onto Reggie's tailored made trousers.

"I'm sorry, really sorry. I'll pay to have them cleaned. I'll loan you a pair of my Levis for now. They will fit you. They are comfortable and when they get dirty you can wash them."

"No thanks, I have another pair of pants, but thanks for the offer," Reggie said.

"I really don't mind," Harry said. Reggie patted him on the shoulder and said, "I'm OK. I'll check you out tomorrow." Reggie started to place his soiled pants on a hanger. He couldn't remember seeing any other student in clothes that resembled his. All they seemed to wear were Levi jeans, sweat shirts, tennis shoes and sport shirts. He thought about Robert, but could not remember how he dressed; however, he was certain Robert was no role model for what to wear. The days of Levi jeans were when he was in grade school. Jeans were definitely not what you wore in Reggie's neighborhood these days if you wanted to be noticed. Everybody he knew worked hard to be able to afford tailor made pants. He had mowed many lawns, distributed hundreds of grocery store flyers, and delivered many newspapers to pay for his wardrobe. Now everybody around him was wearing Levi jeans. He thought for a moment that maybe he should take Harry up on his offer to let him borrow a pair. No way, too embarrassing, he thought.

Just as Reggie was about to turn out the lights and go to bed there was a knock on the door. When he opened it there stood Harry. Before Reggie could say anything, Harry threw a pair of Levis on the bed and headed down the hall without speaking a word. Reggie stood there for a moment speechless. He started to march right up to Harry's room and throw the jeans back at him. *Does he think I am a welfare case that needs his handouts? My pants cost twice as much as his Levis.* Reggie picked up the jeans and began to inspect them. They seemed like they would fit and he thought maybe he could buy a Davis sweatshirt to go with them. He began to think everything Harry had done so far seemed like an attempt to be friendly. So maybe he should make a friendly move by accepting the jeans until he was able to go out and buy his own.

Reggie's only class on Wednesday was eleven o'clock math which he was beginning to see as a humiliation free zone. He had received the result of his first pop quiz: "B." When class was over, he decided to stop by the student union before returning to the dorm. When he entered the cafeteria, he noticed to his right, in a sea of whiteness, a table with only Negro students. It was Nancy and Sandra and they seemed to be engaged in subdued conversation. He headed to the table. He felt embarrassed to see how they were so obviously separated, but glad for the opportunity to consort with other Negroes. They looked in his direction and smiled. Reggie took that as a welcoming gesture. They greeted him and continued their discussion about classes and teachers. Neither of them had the same professors he had. They mimicked their teachers in a manner which implied contempt for some of them. At times they would pause; their faces would grow very serious and they would bite their bottom lip, but they never mentioned a personal negative racial experience in Reggie's presence. At first Reggie was jealous. He was beginning to feel maybe the prejudice he experienced was just directed at him. Maybe they treated Negro women better or maybe the girls just weren't comfortable sharing their feelings with him.

Nancy turned to Reggie and asked, "How are things going on campus?" It hadn't been his intention but Reggie let it all roll out. He described his experience at the fraternity house, Dr. Schulman's reactions, Professor Woodcliff's speech, his lack of a roommate, the isolation he had felt and the incident relating to Robert and Julia.

Nancy said sarcastically, "I thought you would be living the life after being escorted into the freshman dance surrounded by pretty white girls."

Reggie shot back, "Well you thought wrong." He deliberately did not mention Harry. He wanted to muster sympathy from them; however, their only response was, "What a shame."

Sandra shifted the conversation to Robert and Julia. She turned up her nose, shook her head and declared Robert should have known something like that was bound to happen and he could be sure that it was not over. She predicted Robert would be gone before the end of the year. "I wondered if I needed to loan him a mirror," she said snidely. Reggie was disappointed with their attitude. They had not come aboard his train of resentment. When he got up to leave, Nancy looked at his outfit. "Levi jeans and a Davis sweat shirt, looks like you have gotten into the groove of things rather quickly."

"How about that?" Reggie said with a tinge of defiance.

When Reggie was leaving the student union he ran into Robert.

"What's happening?" Robert asked.

"I am on my way back to the dorm."

"I'll walk with you. Man, this place is something else. Some of those girls from Julia's dorm look at me like I am a class project they are studying for a term paper. Some of the guys react to me like I just took a hit from a skunk. Yours is the first friendly face I have come in contact with all day. I haven't heard a word from Julia. I talked to my mom and she said Julia's mother has turned cold on her. She has been telling people Julia caught some virus and had to come home." Robert suddenly realized Reggie was wearing Levi jeans and a Davis sweatshirt. "Hey man what happened to those fancy pants you been wearing. You look like a converted Davis man."

Reggie was embarrassed, but quickly shot back, "They are very comfortable and don't cost as much to keep clean. You should try them."

"What are you doing this evening?" Robert asked.

"Nothing in particular".

"I'll bring down a few LPs and we can listen to some music and maybe forget about this place for a while."

Reggie said that he was willing to give anything a try.

Robert arrived around eight o'clock with Ray Charles, Jackie Wilson, James Brown, Sam Cooke and Jerry Butler. He claimed he needed to feel the music and he turned up the volume. He closed his eyes and leaned back on the bed as Ray Charles sang "Georgia on My Mind." He popped his fingers and tapped his feet to James Brown's "I Feel Good." The music touched Reggie's soul and he swayed in rhythm although he thought the volume was higher than necessary.

In the middle of Sam Cooke's, "Change Gonna Come," there was a knock on the door. When Reggie opened it, his first reaction was to step back to avoid the fire that was bound to come out of the nostrils that were facing him. A chubby white student with a crew cut and thick glasses barked, "This is not Deal Street. Turn that music down. Some of us want to study." Reggie was stunned. Robert leaped to his feet with enough anger to squeeze the life out of the grand dragon of the Ku Klux Klan. Reggie pushed him back before he could say anything and closed the door in the student's face. For a moment Robert increased the volume, but Reggie asked him to lower it.

"That's what I mean when I said this place is something else and I am beginning to realize I am not non violent," Robert said.

In the midst of their venting, there was another knock on the door. They both tensed up ready for a physical confrontation Reggie opened the door. Harry stood in the doorway smiling until he saw the look on Reggie's face. Harry asked what was going on. Reggie quickly regained his composure and said, "Nothing, nothing come in." When Harry saw Robert he stepped back. Reggie noticed the surprised look then said, "This is Robert, a friend of mine from Olive Branch. He lives on the fourth floor." Harry knew Robert was the guy who got the girl kicked out of school before she could start, but he pretended they were meeting for the first time. He looked uncomfortable but sat down anyway.

Robert began bragging about how he was elected captain of his high school debating team, about the team's many triumphs, about the scholarships he turned down to come to Davis, and how he planned to be a lawyer. It all seemed exaggerated. Reggie was embarrassed and irritated. After about fifteen minutes Harry's excused himself by saying that he had to finish an essay for class tomorrow. Reggie wanted Robert to follow Harry so he could cool down and get some sleep, but Robert wasn't about to leave before getting the scoop on Harry.

Reggie explained that Harry was in his gym class, they had talked several times, and he seemed like a good guy. He neglected to mention it was Harry who gave him the information about Julia's expulsion.

"If you say he is OK, then he is OK with me," Robert quipped.

13

No matter how hard Reggie tried, he could never get more than a C— from Dr. Schulman and he became more and more certain as the semester trailed along that race was the sole factor infecting Dr. Schulman's grading system. Dr. Woodcliff, however, presented a more frightening situation.

He had announced at the beginning of the year that he only gave two tests during the semester, a mid term and a final, and required two papers, and the grade would be based on these factors only. He returned Reggie's first paper with no red marks but with a grade of "D" and the comment; "Your conclusions were not supported by sufficient research." Reggie made several attempts to see him during his advertised counseling hours to discuss his comment, but he always told Reggie he would have to come back at a later time because he was busy even though there was no one in his office or in the waiting area. Reggie felt helpless. There was no place to turn and without some understanding of exactly what Dr. Woodcliff was looking for he felt doomed. He didn't want to go to the dean to complain and be labeled an ignorant Negro unable to adjust to Davis standards. He also began to have doubts about his abilities and the quality of his schooling. Maybe his education in an all Negro school had imbued him with a false sense of confidence. The white students did seem more confident. He was reluctant to speak up in class, because all eyes would be on him the second they heard his voice.

Dr. Caton and Dr. Thorn's classes saved him from a complete descent into self doubt. His work was averaging a "B" in both classes; however, he sometimes wondered if Dr. Thorn was just being nice to him because she probably understood what he was experiencing in some of his other classes.

Indian summer passed and fall set in. The campus glowed in bright red, pale yellow, rusty gold and rich orange colored leaves clinging to those trees wantonly awaiting their new birth. The streams of cool air descending from the north mandated an additional layer of clothing to be comfortable outside. Weeks were filled with excitement about each Saturday's football game as the Davis Panthers continued their winning streak. Reggie couldn't help being drawn into the hoopla since he loved football and so did Robert. They went to all the games and cheered as loudly as any other student. This period also marked the onset of midterm exams, the first real test of Reggie's survival. To prepare for this showdown, he spent most of his free time in a quiet, private spot he had found in the library.

Reggie walked into Dr. Schulman's class with his fingers crossed. The test had both multiple choice and essay questions, and he felt he knew the answers to all of them.

Dr. Woodcliff's test was all essay, which was unsettling; however, he was confident he had command of the material and, if judged fairly, he should score high enough to end up with at least a "C".

He was also confident, at least, that he passed his math test, and that the tests for psychology, American History and Physical Education were breezes.

I should now be on track in getting that education that I have been told endless times, "the white man can't take away from you", if prejudice professors don't stand in my way, he declared. I wish the justices on the Supreme Court had added something to their decision about how Negroes should be treated *after* they were allowed in previously all white schools.

14

WITH MIDTERMS A THING OF THE PAST, REGGIE DECLARED IT TIME TO celebrate. His first thought was to write Mona, but decided that was something for tomorrow. He needed to let go of some steam. Maybe Robert and Harry also needed to escape and wouldn't mind going into town. Robert answered the door after the first knock and with great enthusiasm joined Reggie. The two went and knocked on Harry's door. Harry's first reaction was a hearty hello, but when he saw Robert he thanked Reggie for the invitation, but said he still had to complete a paper for his class in European History.

Robert and Reggie found their way to the Negro section in town by chasing the smell of fried fish. When they walked into the restaurant, it felt like a family reunion. Negroes were all over the place and no one looked up to see who they were or waited to hear the first word out of their mouths. The waitress walked over and asked, "What can I get for you two handsome men? Y'all look like you are from Davis."

Robert leaned back in his chair and said, "You are looking at two Davis University scholars making a move into town for the first time. What do you have for us?"

"Well welcome to town, Davis scholars. We have some down home food we are sure you haven't had since you arrived at Davis. Now take this menu and swim in it. I'll be back in a minute to fish you out." Reading the menu was like meeting old friends. There were pork chops, spare ribs, smothered chicken, catfish, collard greens, potato salad, macaroni and cheese, corn bread and biscuits. It was hard to choose since all those dishes had been noticeably absent from the choices they had over the past few months. They finally decided to indulge themselves in some fried catfish, potato salad, collard greens and hot corn bread, topped off with sweet ice tea. Reggie claimed the greens were good but not as good as his mother's. Robert swore his mother's potato salad was the best in the South; but he would give this one a "B".

The juke box was pumping out Jerry Butler, John Lee Hooker, Johnny Mathis and The Drifters' while Reggie and Robert hummed and tapped their feet in rhythm with the beat. The music went silent for a minute and someone dropped another quarter in the jukebox and out rolled a deep melodious voice sounding like Arthur Prysock singing, "You never close your eyes when I kiss your lips ...." Robert and Reggie closed their eyes and began to rock. Robert asked Reggie, "Who are they and what's the name of that song?

"I never heard it before," Reggie admitted.

"Hey, foxy mama, who are those crooners?" Robert yelled across the room to the waitress. "I thought I knew all the latest Negro recording artists."

"Well, you might have," the waitress said. "The song is called 'You've Lost That Loving Feeling' and the group is the Righteous Brothers and they are not Negroes."

"Stop pulling my leg! You are kidding!" Robert shouted.

"I'm not kidding, but whenever you are ready I'll pull your leg." The waitress said as she rushed off to the next table.

"Name the place and time and I'll be there leg and all," Robert answered.

"Man, can you believe your ears? We are doomed. They are not only going to kick us out of their schools but they are going to claim our music. Maybe we need to go back to the Supreme Court and see if we can get them convicted for stealing our music."

After dinner Robert suggested they try their hand at getting a sip of alcohol. They tried two bars and were summarily asked to leave. They decided to change their strategy and wait until they identified a friendly face of the right age and ask the person to purchase some for them. It didn't take long to spot this man sitting in the park alone in clothes that seemed to have been with him for days. He told them he would gladly oblige but they had to buy some for him.

Reggie and Robert headed back to the park where they downed their beer faster than they should have. Reggie felt in control of his faculties, but Robert was struggling to stand and had stopped making sense. He began to drift off into a state of melancholy. He bemoaned his academic performance and insisted that he wouldn't be able to make it at Davis, especially after what he had done to Julia. Reggie shared his experiences with Dr. Schulman and Dr. Woodcliff, but it didn't seem to matter to Robert. Reggie looked at his watch and realized it was eleven o'clock and they had missed the last bus back to campus. With no experience in town, he wasn't sure what their options were.

"Let's go man, it's late and we have to find a way back to campus, the buses have stopped running." Robert staggered up and managed enough equilibrium to walk without assistance. Reggie decided they should walk towards the bus station. He remembered there were taxis lined up outside the station when he arrived in town, and maybe they could still get one back to campus. As they walked towards the station a taxi drove up beside them and the driver asked, "Where are you boys headed?"

Davis University, sir," Reggie said.

"Get in, I'm going that way." The driver beckoned them.

"Thank you sir! Thank you," Reggie said. It didn't take a minute for him to recognize the driver. He was the one that drove him to campus that first day.

The driver also recognized Reggie and asked, "How is it going for you guys out there?"

The question had a slight sobering effect on Robert. He jumped into the conversation with slurred speech and spilled the whole history of his struggle at Davis. Reggie didn't feel it necessary to add anything. The driver listened in silence as Robert laid out his pain.

When he finished, the driver began, "I want you guy to be careful out there. Davis can be a dangerous place for Negroes. My son was a student there last year and was attacked by a group of students in white sheets last Halloween as he was leaving the library. They broke his nose. Nothing was ever done. The administration claimed it was Halloween and there were a lot of pranks that night and they could not identify the students responsible. The NAACP protested but couldn't come up with any names to present to the school. We took Carl out of there. There just weren't any protections for him. You know there is a rumor the president is a member of the John Birch Society, which is as close to the Ku Klux Klan as you can get when it comes to blocking civil rights for Negroes. Make sure you watch out for those white students that make trouble. Try to get their names. There is a professor there named Dr. Elizabeth Thorn. She is a great lady – very fair minded. She once taught at LeMoyne College, that Negro school over in Memphis. Carl had respect for her. If you get a chance to take her class, don't pass it up. She will treat you right. My pastor, Rev. Williams, told me she comes from Atlanta and her best friends growing up were the children of the Negro servants. When her parents tried to force her to socialize with the children of their friends, she would throw tantrums and start fights with the white children. They sent her to a school in Switzerland hoping she would return a refined white girl with good Southern values. Well, they would turn over in their graves if they knew she sold the house which had been in the family for generations and bought one for the Negro housekeeper that had worked for the family for twenty years. She went to college up North, some school called Vassar College and then to Columbia University in New York. She was married to Daniel Thorn, a big shot at Slumber Products who had been transferred from Atlanta. Rev. Williams said she changed him from a staunch southerner to a tolerant southerner. He had a heart attack that killed him and she remained in Danville- many say to be close to him."

"She is my history teacher," Reggie said, but he was having a hard time thinking of anything other than the driver's son.

At the dorm, the driver gave Reggie his telephone number and said, "You can call me if there is anything you think I can do to help you guys." Reggie thanked him, paid the fare, and Robert groveled something that sounded like a thanks.

Reggie laid in bed trying to find sleep, thinking that this was one hell of a place. He wondered if Rosa Parks ever considered giving up that seat and going home to a good meal and a good night's rest; or whether that Dr. King ever thought about just pastoring a congregation that celebrated his anniversary every year with a new Cadillac or some other expensive gift? He wondered if Harriett Tubman ever thought about staying in the north after her first successful trip freeing slaves; or whether the Quakers ever considered not answering their doors when the slaves on the Underground Railroad knocked?

15

MIDTERM GRADES WERE HANDED OUT IN CLASS AND ENGLISH COMPOSITION was Reggie's first. Dr. Schulman entered the lecture hall with a stack of blue test booklets that he plopped down on his desk as if he was greatly relieved. He called the names on each booklet and the students marched to the front of class to receive theirs. Reggie sat with his heart pounding. When his name was called he almost leaped out of his seat and marched to the front with his hands shaking. Dr. Schulman handed him the book and looked down for the next name. Reggie strolled back to his seat with the unopened book feeling the nerve endings all over his body crawling to the surface of this skin. After taking a deep breath, he opened the book and there at the top of the first page was a large bold "C—" the same one that had appeared on all his earlier papers. The rest of the period went by without his attention. He was consumed wondering what was to come in Dr. Woodcliff's class.

By the time English class ended, he had decided he would be prepared for whatever Dr. Woodcliff hurled in his direction. However, when Dr. Woodcliff handed him the Blue Book, and the "D" on the inside of the cover stared at him, he had to hold back the tears. He imagined things wouldn't be any better in his other classes and was tempted to skip them. He needed more time to build strength to face the pain. He walked out of Dr. Woodcliff's class in a daze. Before he realized what he was doing he was at the door of Dr. Caton's class and too embarrassed to turn around. He walked in, emotionally exhausted, unable to muster any more doubts or fears. When Dr. Caton called his name he walked up to her feeling numb. As soon as she handed him the Blue Book, he opened it and discovered a "C". He felt a glimmer of hope and enough optimism to face his other classes. He received a "C+" in math, a "B+" in American History, and "B" in Physical Education. Thank you God for cracking a window after the devil slammed two doors in my face, he prayed. He was relieved but not happy. Those grades would not permit him to maintain his scholarship.

When Dr. Thorn gave Reggie his exam she also handed him an envelope and told him she hoped he would be able to join her. He opened the envelope as soon as he returned to his seat. It was an invitation to a reception for the actors in a road show of the play, "A Raisin in the Sun." Reggie had never been to a reception, except the ones for parents and teachers at Booker T. Washington and the only plays he had ever seen were those put on at school. In spite of his apprehensions, he realized this was an invitation that couldn't be turned down. Dr. Thorn had reached out to him and he was badly in need of friendly faces. At the end of class he told her he would be there.

Thoughts of the reception dominated Reggie's thinking until it was time to go. One thing he felt secure about was that he was not going to show up in blue jeans and a sweatshirt. A pair of those tailor made pants and a coordinated shirt were definitely coming off those hangers in his closet. When he arrived, Dr. Thorn greeted him with a warm smile and thanked him for coming. She asked how he was doing adjusting to life at Davis.

"I'm doing OK," Reggie answered as he tried to look past her to see who was in the crowd. She then inquired about what classes he was taking. He rattled off his classes and named the professors without any editorial comment, even though something inside of him was saying he should go into details with her but he didn't trust that feeling. Dr. Thorn commented that adjusting to college is often more challenging to students than they anticipated, especially if it is the first time they are leaving home. She encouraged him to develop a resolve to succeed and then work hard and everything would work out.

My God, he thought. She probably knows everything that's happening to me. He assured her he would work hard and thanked her for the advice as he bowed his head and looked towards the floor. She then took him around and introduced him. There were several white couples but most of the crowd was Negroes. They looked like the group at Mona's debutante's ball and they acted pretty much the same. They smiled when he was introduced and then returned to their conversations. When Reggie was introduced to the cast, which had only one white person, he concluded the play had to be about Negroes. He was relieved and began to feel comfortable. The actors were very friendly. They questioned him about his background and what he was studying. He proudly announced he was a freshman from Smoky Mountain and told them the courses he was taking.

"What do the people back in Smoky Mountain think of you?" one of the actors asked. "My parents are happy for me," Reggie said. Their conversation was interrupted by the ringing of the door bell. When the door opened and the person entered, Reggie's heart missed a beat. It was Betty, looking good enough to eat, in a blue dress clinging to that beautiful body and her blond hair flowing around her shoulders. His blood began to take a detour to his crotch. He took several deep breaths and then sipped his cold drink. Once he felt back in control, he was embarrassed and hoped no one was able to read his mind. There wasn't much time to wonder. Dr. Thorn was heading towards him with Betty at her side.

"Mr. Morton, I would like to introduce you to Betty Duvall, a classmate of yours," Reggie didn't know whether he should acknowledge he knew Betty, considering what happened to Julia. But she had no such reservations.

"Yes, I met Mr. Morton before on campus," Betty said. Dr. Thorn looked a bit surprised, but smiled and continued to introduce Betty to her other guests. A white couple quickly co-opted Betty into their animated conversation. Betty kept looking towards Reggie and the cast. At the first opportunity she meandered back to them.

She and Reggie began talking about their classes and the football team. Reggie kept looking to see if anyone was watching them. Several of the Negroes did turn their heads in their direction, but it seemed more out of curiosity than disapproval. Reggie was still uncomfortable. He kept thinking about what happened when he saw Betty walk in the door and now he began to feel unfaithful to Mona. There was also the Robert/Julia scenario that added to his discomfort. He noticed people were beginning to leave, and decided that that was his cue to head out.

He told Betty he thought it was time for him to head back to the dorm, but he wanted to say good bye to the actors before he left. Betty just smiled at him as he walked away. The actors hugged him and wished him luck and said they hoped to see him at the play. Reggie approached Dr. Thorn and told her how much he appreciated the invitation and how much he enjoyed the evening. She handed him an envelope with two tickets. When he realized what they were, he took her hand, thanked her and told her how much he looked forward to seeing the play. He walked out of the house feeling relieved that he had made it through the reception without embarrassing himself.

When he was half a block away from Dr. Thorn's house, he heard a voice call, "Hold up. I'm going your way." It was Betty. Reggie was knocked off balance. Sweat began to form around his neck, trailing down his back, landing at the tip of his spine and further awakening activity in his crotch. He wanted to continue their friendly conversation, but was afraid. This was not a good place to be alone with a white girl. "Good Lord, please send this woman rushing past me," he prayed. He turned around and tried to force a smile through his nervous lips. He could feel his nature rising and hoped the darkness would hide it. He prayed again under his breath, "Please, God, don't let these prejudiced folks see us." But at the same time the dark deserted street with dimly lit houses deeply recessed behind spacious lawns or clusters of trees made him think of the possibilities.

In an effort to appear composed, he asked Betty if she took a course from Dr. Thorn. Betty explained that she was in her other

American History class. She also told him that her parents had known Dr. Thorn for a long time. She and her mother had been classmates at Vassar. Reggie noticed that as they walked Betty continued to bump into him for no good reason. Reggie's heartbeat went into high gear and he longed for this stroll to be over. After a while they found themselves in a block where the street lights were out. The darkness was only interrupted by the dim lights from the next block. Without a word of warning, Betty leaned towards Reggie and kissed him on the cheek. Reggie's nature rolled over his fear and he landed one on her lips. Her arms wrapped around his neck and embraced him passionately. As he felt her body next to his and her soft lips indulging his tongue, a moment of ecstasy jolted his whole body and caused him to tremble and a shower of joy released itself into his jockey shorts. The moment of joy was short lived. Reggie was embarrassed and scared. He prayed again, "Lord, if you help me out of this, I promise to never put myself in this kind of situation again." He turned away from Betty. She knew what had happened, but did not acknowledge it.

Reggie spoke up, saying, "We had better get back." Betty said nothing as Reggie pulled away from her. The rest of the walk they were both silent. Once Betty reached for Reggie's hand but he pulled it away. When they were about two blocks from campus, Reggie said, "I think I had better walk ahead."

Betty answered, "I look forward to seeing you on campus and the next time we can be alone."

Reggie looked away as the words, "I'll see you," escaped his lips. He increased his pace and arrived in his room with a bundle of conflicting feelings and soiled underwear. The first thing he had to do was to take a shower.

While in the shower he tried to focus on how he would handle the situation if someone saw them and how he would handle Betty the next time he saw her. Those thoughts, however, would not stick and his mind kept wandering back to the fantasy of having sex with Betty in an unthreatening environment and each time the thought crept back, he became excited again. He hurried out of the shower hoping no one would see him. He tried to go to sleep. As he reached to turn out the light on his desk trying to find sleep, his hand touched an envelope. It was the letter from Mona.

After holding the letter to his chest for a minute, Reggie finally opened it. Mona spoke positively about what was going on with her and talked about how much she missed him and how much she looked forward to Christmas when they could be together. Reggie felt rotten. He had betrayed the love of his life. He wondered how he would explain this to her. He needed to talk to someone before he spilled his guts to Mona. Robert was out of the question. Surely, he would think Reggie was out of his mind considering what had already happened to him. Harry was white and that made him an even less likely candidate. Reggie decided to sleep on it.

The next morning Reggie was thinking much more clearly. Kissing Betty was not the worst incident in the world. After all it was just a kiss. He wouldn't tell Mona or anyone else and he had no intention of letting it happen again. Maintaining a comfortable distance from Betty would take care of everything.

Reggie's thoughts turned to the two tickets he had to "A Raisin in he Sun." He wondered what he would do with the extra one. Of course Betty was out of the question. Robert was likely to embarrass him and he didn't want Nancy to think that he was interested in her, so that left only Harry. *But what if the audience were all Negro. How would that make Harry feel? Well, at least he would know I am trying to be his friend.*

When Reggie asked Harry he emphasized Dr. Thorn had given him the tickets and he made no mention of the reception or the race of the cast. Harry quickly agreed without any questions.

The night of the show, Harry wore his Levis with a sport shirt, but put on a jacket. Reggie wore a suit and tie. The theater was in a high school auditorium with a spacious stage and dark red velvet curtains and hard wooden seats. It was crowded with mostly Negroes, but there were a few more whites than were at the reception. Dr. Thorn was there with some of the people Reggie recognized from the reception. After saying hello to her, Reggie and Harry followed the usher to their seats. Harry's hand shook as he turned the pages of the program, keeping his head down. Reggie prayed the play would not last long and was glad he had on a jacket because he could feel sweat forming on his back. Reggie raised his head from the program and looked towards the audience trying to pretend he didn't notice Harry. His shirt began to cling to the sweat on his back. Two rows ahead of him sat Betty and two of the girls that escorted him into the freshman dance. He wondered if Betty had told the girls what happened to him.Half way into the first act the theme of the play was strikingly clear and Reggie declared it was not going to be a pleasant evening. There on stage for everybody to see was a poor Negro family washing their lives before a mixed audience and there he was watching it with a white boy. He cringed as he saw that the family relationships and their problems on stage were all familiar to him. He had no sympathy for the son who squandered his father's life insurance on a scheme that wiped out the money for his sister's college education and left his mother with a house in a restricted white neighborhood where she had only made a down payment. Reggie compared him to the hoodlums in his neighborhood. Harry did not know how to comment on the play. He didn't want to say something stupid or that would offend Reggie so they both sat silently as it progressed.When the curtains fell for intermission, Reggie's chief concern was how to avoid Betty. As soon as the audience began to applaud, Reggie leaned over to Harry and said, "Let's get a drink." He figured if they moved early, the crowd would put a distance between them and Betty and her friends. As they stood waiting in line at the concession stand, there was a tap on Reggie's shoulder. Suddenly his mouth went dry. He turned around and there was Betty looking him directly in the eyes. He pretended he was surprised and said, "Betty, What are you doing here? How are you enjoying the play?" As soon as those words were out of his mouth, he wanted to kick himself. God knows he didn't want to talk about the play.

"I was given tickets the other night at the reception. You remember Charlotte and Lacey." Reggie said hello to them and turned to introduce Harry who looked as flustered as the contestant on the popular TV show who was asked to spell antidisestablishmentarianism but managed a smile and shook their hands. Reggie ordered two Pepsis, handed one to Harry, and said, "It was good seeing you all again," and then walked away. Betty looked at him somewhat confused and then winked slyly, causing the muscles in Reggie's back to tighten. He was glad Harry did not see it.

Throughout the rest of the play Reggie planned how not to run into Betty again. When the audience began to clap after the last act and before the actors came out for their bow, Reggie abruptly said to Harry, "Let's go. It's late and I have to review a couple of chapters before my history class tomorrow."

They exited through a side door close to their seats and headed for the street leading to the campus. Harry didn't want to talk about the play any more than Reggie. As soon as they were on the street he said, "I think I will sign up for Dr. Thorn's American History class next semester. I hear she is an excellent teacher and that the rest of the faculty don't like her, but she's got tenure and is well respected in her field so they can't get rid of her."

"She is the best teacher I have this semester. I think you will like her. How do you know so much about her?" Reggie asked. Harry explained his big brother on campus gave him the low down on as many professors as he knew about. Reggie asked, "How did you find a big brother so fast?"

"He is a sophomore and was assigned to me during orientation," Harry explained.

"No one offered to assign me a big brother," Reggie said. To change the subject, Harry hurriedly asked Reggie if he had ever been to Chicago. Reggie hesitated for a moment while he absorbed the hurt from the slap he had just been handed.

"No, I haven't."

"Well, you have to see it," said Harry. "There are always things to do and places to go. Its heaven compared to Danville. There is no such thing as closing down town at five o'clock. We rock through the night," Harry said. "I'm going some day. I've always wanted to see it, but have never had the chance."

"You'll love it. There's no way anyone wouldn't love it," Harry bragged. By now they had reached the dorm. Harry thanked Reggie for the tickets and they went their separate ways.

Back in his room, Reggie let out a deep sigh. Now was a good time to write to Mona. Her letters had been coming less frequently, but he still owed her one. As he sat at his desk trying to decide where to start, Betty's face flashed in his mind and he remembered the explosion his body experienced the other night when they kissed. The thought caused his nature to rise. It would not retreat so he was forced to rethink his priorities at the moment and attend to a more pressing matter.

The next morning was a Saturday so Reggie stayed in his bed with the blanket pulled over him. It was one of those fall days with overcast skies, cool temperature and vigorous winds. From his bed he could see the trees that had lost their leaves to the howling winds and pouring rain and now stood bare. As he lay there gazing out the window, he thought about the beautiful blossoms that would return to the trees in the spring. He wanted to feel optimistic, but it seemed there was an outside force controlling his thoughts. He tried to think of those happy days in high school, but the only thought he could muster was the message Rev. Bailey gave at the baccalaureate service, "If you can take it you can make it." He wondered if Rev. Bailey would have said that if he had to actually live with prejudiced white people every day. He then thought about Harry and Dr. Thorn, the "Bs" he got at mid term, how proud his parents were that he was at Davis and how much Mona loved him.

Reggie rolled out of bed, went directly to his desk and began the letter to Mona. Suddenly feeling invincible, he vowed again there would never be a repeat of the incident with Betty. She could be a threat to his future. It would be harder if he didn't have someone that loved him, but he had Mona. Anyway, he was a man and things like that happen to men. We lose control sometimes when it comes to women, but we have the power to recoup. So he wrote Mona that things were going well and he hoped to hear from her soon.

16

When Reggie was finishing gym class on Monday, Harry hurried over to him and said, "Wait for me when you come out of the shower. I need to talk to you about something."

Reggie was hoping that Harry had some more inside dope about another professor. "I hope it's Dr. Schulman or Woodcliff," he thought. "I would love to know what makes those two crackers tick."

"Are you planning to go home for the Thanksgiving break," Harry asked.

"No. I'm going home for Christmas. I can't afford to do both."

"Well, my family would like to have you join us in Chicago, all expenses paid.

We could take the train from Memphis that Tuesday afternoon before Thanksgiving after classes and get to Chicago on Wednesday morning. I think we would have a great time. My mother wants to meet you and if you're not going home she is going to insist that you come. How about it?" Reggie's head began to spin.

He needed to contain his enthusiasm until all the details had been laid out. What did Harry tell his mother that made her want to meet me? He wanted to ask. Harry stood with a big smile waiting for his glee to be reciprocated.

"I don't know, buddy," slowly rolled off Reggie lips. The idea of going to Chicago was the most exciting thing he had thought about in a long time. It was the place most of the people he knew always talked about visiting. He would have so much to brag about when he went home for Christmas which might save him from giving too many details about life at Davis. He was sure Harry could see the smile struggling to get through, but he wanted to think more before accepting. "Let me think about it," he said finally.

"I know you will have a great time. So think positive. Thanksgiving is next week so you need to let me know as soon as possible so my mother can get the tickets. She will be really disappointed if you don't come," Harry pleaded.

That afternoon, Reggie tried to think of some reasons he shouldn't take this trip, but his mind made no room for doubts. Excitement overpowered him. He realized he had to notify his parents and there was not enough time to write a letter and get an answer, so he rang them. He had never called them on the phone before so when Mrs. Morton answered the phone and when she heard Reggie's voice she sounded both happy and frightened.

"Hey son, how are you? It is so good to hear your voice. Is everything all right?"

"Mom everything is fine. I told you about my good grades after mid term exams and so far I'm keeping up the good works. Oh, mom I went to see a play called, "A Raisin in the Sun" about a poor Negro family in Chicago. One of my professors, Dr. Thorn, gave me the tickets and invited me to her house to meet the actors. I had a great time. I don't want to spend all my money on this telephone call so let me get to the point. Harry, a guy I met here, has invited me to go home with him for Thanksgiving. His parents invited me and they want to give me an all expenses paid trip to Chicago. What do you think?" Mrs. Morton was stunned by the question. Nervously, she asked, "Do you know him well enough to visit his home? I assume they are white. Are they rich? What kind of neighborhood do they live in? Make sure you don't run into those street gangs. They are dangerous. Do you have money to spend when you get there? Make sure your clothes are clean. When was the last time you got a hair cut? Take Cousin Ellie's telephone number and address in case something happens. We haven't spoken in a long time but she will remember you. Tell her everybody is doing fine and I have been intending to write but have been so busy, but I will soon." She was almost out of breath when her last comments rolled out. She had always wanted to visit Chicago herself and would love to tell everyone about Reggie's trip there.

With his mother's approval, Reggie began to feel Chicago was in his reach. He was embarrassed about Harry's family paying for the ticket but realized that if they didn't he wouldn't be able to go. His mind began buzzing. They must be rich like the folks at the country club where he once worked. Would they have Negro neighbors or just Negro servants? This, he realized, was his opportunity to really see up close how white folks do it, but the thought still made him nervous.

The next day Reggie accepted Harry's invitation. He grabbed Reggie's hand, shook it vigorously and said, "You won't regret it."

Robert stopped by Reggie's room the Saturday before Thanksgiving to announce that he would be leaving for the holiday on Monday evening if he could finish his paper on time. Reggie requested that he bring him back some good soul food. Robert assumed Reggie was staying on campus and Reggie made no effort to reveal his plans. He felt a bit guilty, but was not ready to explain his growing relationship with Harry. He didn't want to alienate Robert who Reggie thought was still nursing his wounds from the way he lost Julia.The week-end went by quickly. Reggie had a list of assignments due before the break so he was racing to complete them. Before he knew it, Monday was there and he was leaving the next day for Chicago. He was full of excitement. It reminded him of Christmas Eve when he and Doug would pull out the shoe box they had been storing under the bed since September when their annual pair of shoes arrived in the mail from Sears Roebucks. They would write their names on the boxes so Santa Claus would know whose box was whose. Mrs. Morton would chase them to bed around eight o'clock and warn them if they stayed awake Santa Claus would put ashes in their box instead of presents. They would jump in bed and close their eyes tightly, fighting to go to sleep. When they awoke it was usually still dark and they were afraid to go and see if Santa had come, but after a while, curiosity overcame fear and they charged to the front room and there in their boxes were oranges, apples, raisins, nuts, candy and a toy. Doug would often get a box of fireworks and head for the yard to set them off, echoing into the distance. Reggie remembered the Christmas he got a small blue boat that he placed in the washing tub and watched sail while Doug set off firecrackers.

As Reggie selected his clothes for the trip, he found himself whistling Gloria Lynn's, "Our Day Will Come". He smiled when he got to the part that said, "...and we will have everything." It was a sleepless night and an anxious morning. He went to math, his only class, but had no idea what was covered. When class was over, he rushed back to his room to wait for Harry.

Twenty minutes later there were three taps on Reggie's door: the Harry Dubinsky trademark. Reggie looked in the mirror, checking that his Caesar haircut was perfect. He looked at that old worn out leather suitcase with tattered straps buckled at the top, shook his head and said, "What the hell."

Reggie swung open the door. Harry was leaning on the door frame. He was dressed in his suburban coat, a stocking cap pulled down over his ears, a long scarf curving around his neck and trailing down his coat to his leather fur lined gloves. He looked like someone ready for a spin in the North Pole. "Well, buddy, are you ready to venture north for the time of your life?"

Reggie wondered if his waist-length coat, bibbed cap and wool gloves were enough for Chicago. He had heard of people getting frost bite on crucial parts of their anatomy and he suddenly feared coming back to Smoky Mountain unable to father children. He wondered if he should have brought his long johns. Maybe, but what if someone saw the bottoms connecting with his socks. They would quickly brand him a hick from the South.

"I am ready to see if your Chicago is just one big greasy spot on the map or God's gift to a lonely man."Harry threw his duffle bag over his shoulder. Reggie picked up the old suitcase and the two headed for the bus that would take them to the train station in Memphis. Reggie remembered all the times he had heard the lonely sound of a train's whistle as it passed through Smoky

Mountain on its way to some unknown, exotic destination. He fantasized traveling like the people in the circus and going to New York City or Los Angeles, California and seeing the Pacific Ocean and the Empire State Building and returning home to brag about his exploits.

The train station was at the end of Main Street perched on top of a hill overlooking the city. You could see its tall columns a half mile away. It looked like the pictures of the front of plantation houses in slavery times, except its roof was curved and made of what looked like concrete. The sight of it made Reggie a little nervous. He pictured slaves, maybe his great grandparents, coming in from the fields to the Big House to see what bad news the Massa had for them this time.

When they reached the station, Reggie saw travelers milling around with stressed looks on their faces; children tugging at their parents and demanding attention. There was a handful of elderly Negro men and women with children. Next to them was a host of Negro men dressed in dark navy blue suits with shining brass buttons down the front asking people if they needed any help with their luggage. As Harry held the door for Reggie, a voice called out, "Hey, boy, come take these bags for me." Reggie hesitated. The call was surely meant for one of the Negroes in dark blue suits and he was wearing a brown coat."Did you hear me, boy? I am talking to you." Reggie noticed a Negro woman and her child looking at him. He turned and there, pointing a cane in his face, was an elderly humped-over white man with white hair crawling from under a black fedora. The man looked Reggie straight in the eyes and tapped the bags with his cane. Automatically, Reggie reached for the bags.

Harry grabbed his hand, looked at the old man and said, "He doesn't work here.'

Reggie's felt he had been striped of all his clothes. I must have looked like a runaway slave captured by bounty hunters. Thank God, Arnold couldn't see me, he thought. He would never let me live it down. I should have told that old cracker to kiss my black ass and to ask his mama to carry his damn bags. Who the hell does he think I am? I am a freshman at Davis University, the school he probably flunked out of.

Harry walked ahead as if nothing had happened. Finally, he stopped in front of the marquee of arrivals and departures. Reggie stood directly behind him in the restless crowd wondering if he should thank Harry, apologize, or what? Beads of sweat began popping on his forehead. As he raised his hand to make them disappear, the clicking sound of train notification postings startled him. He looked up and there on the board under destinations: Chicago, New Orleans, Atlanta, Washington, D.C., New York. He began to fantasize seeing himself dancing down Bourbon Street in New Orleans to the jazz sounds flowing out of the bars; climbing the steps of the Supreme Court building in Washington, D.C.; or dressed in a three piece suit, open shirt with an ascot around his neck strolling into the Apollo theater in New York that he had heard so much about. Looking around at the travelers, he began imagining their various destinations. A Negro woman with two children must be off to Atlanta to visit her ill sister. A lone Negro man was headed for New Orleans to pursue his fantasies of a good time in the wild French Quarter. A white couple in very fashionable dress was surely destined for New York and the bright lights of Broadway and Times Square. The old white man he had just encountered must be making a connection for his home in the delta of Mississippi where the servants called him 'Massa.'

"Our train seems to be on time, but they haven't posted a track yet. Let's go find a seat in the waiting area." Harry walked them into a spacious room with high ceilings and hard wooden benches lined up in rows on two sides of the marble floor. There was poor light trickling from the light bulbs on the ceiling. The room was filled with travelers dressed as if they were on their way to Sunday church services. The women were covered in fur coats, wool coats with fur around the collars or just plain wool. The men sported dark grey or black three quarter length overcoats, fedoras and leather gloves. Their shoes sparkled from recent shines. Children broke away from their parents and ran up and down the aisles laughing and shouting.

Reggie noticed the Negroes were huddled on two benches in the back of the room. The women were sitting with their backs straight, their gloved hands resting in their laps, ankles touching, heads held erect as if they remembered posture taught in Mrs. Foster's finishing school. They held their children's hands tightly and whispered to them as the children struggled to free themselves. The men crossed and uncrossed their legs at frequent intervals, seemingly as restless as the children.

Harry led Reggie to a bench three rows in front of the Negroes. On one side of them was a white woman with a child and on the other were two white men who appeared to be traveling together. They shifted slightly, though there was plenty of room, and looked at Reggie and frowned. Harry plopped down his duffle as if he owned the bench. He sat down, leaned back, spread his legs, closed his eyes and exhaled.

"It's not always like this. A lot of people travel at Thanksgiving and the train people are never prepared for the crowds." The bus station gets crowded and nerve-racking too," Reggie said. He took the seat next to Harry hoping Harry would not open his eyes and start talking about the incident. However, he wondered what was gong on in Harry's head.

"The six o'clock City of New Orleans to Chicago is loading on track Number 12. All aboard," trumpeted the voice over the microphone.

"Let's go, buddy. That's us. Reggie again trailed behind Harry through the gate and down the platform. Harry seemed to be searching for something. There were plenty seats in the coaches they passed. Was there something different about seats in other coaches? Harry finally led them into a coach where they secured their luggage on the rack over their heads and slid down into the firm cloth-covered seats. Reggie looked around. Harry was the only white person in the coach and it was practically full. Harry had purposely led them to that coach probably attempting to make Reggie feel comfortable even though they could have sat any place they wanted, according to the law.

"Is he ashamed to have white people see him with me?" Reggie's mind began to race. "There is no way in the world he could be comfortable here. Look, people are beginning to stare. Didn't he have sense enough to realize this would happen? Has he been living in the North Pole? If he's trying to make me comfortable, now both of us are miserable. With all these stares, I hope he doesn't wet his pants."

"How are you doing buddy?" Harry asked nervously.

"Just fine." Reggie leaned back and closed his eyes tightly wondering how many more lies will he have to tell during this trip.

The conductor entered the coach. He was medium height, stockily built with round narrow shoulders. He looked like Mr. Bob from the neighborhood store.

"Please take out your tickets and have them ready for me as I come to you." The gruff stern voice startled Reggie. Recalling the earlier incident, he decided he was in no mood to tolerate any more insults. As the conductor approached each passenger, he extended his hand, took the ticket, clipped it and placed it in the overhead receptacle without making eye contact. When he reached Reggie and Harry, he looked directly at them winked and said, "Where are you guys going tonight?"

"We're on our way to Chicago. This is my friend's first visit and I promised him a really good time."

"Well, young man, you are in for the time of your life. Chicago has a lot of things to do. I bet you will be itching to come back after this visit." He turned from Reggie to Harry. "You take good care of him and both of you stay out of trouble."

"Yes, sir," Harry nodded stiffly as if he had just heard a military command.

While Reggie tried to relax, Harry began rattling off the high points of Chicago: Wrigley Field, Chicago River, Michigan Ave, the Art Institute, the Loop and Old Town. He went on about how this was going to be one of the best Thanksgivings his family ever had. He sounded like a used car salesman. Reggie was exhausted and began to fall asleep. Hours later when Reggie opened his eyes it was dark. Harry's head was resting on the back of the seat. His eyes were closed and a light snore crept from his open mouth. Reggie felt more relaxed than he had all day. The sound of the train charging over the tracks, the rumble of rapid movement and the occasional sound of the train's whistle were like a lullaby. He gave in to the soft seat and head rest and slept.

Throughout the night his sleep was interrupted by the announcement of an arrival station and the hustle of passengers in and out of the coach. The occasional smell of fried chicken occasionally caught his attention and reminded him that he had not eaten for hours. He drifted back to sleep and began to dream. This time he was at a table covered with a green vinyl cloth. There was a bowl of pinto beans and a pan of hot corn bread. He reached for the food that seemed too far for him to grab. He awoke and then fell back to sleep dreaming about a warm spring day. He rushed out to play "stick" ball with his friends in the alley between their houses. They played until his mother called him in for the evening and ordered him to bed where he knew he would sleep soundly through the night. The dream moved into a cold winter day. Reggie and his friends were gathered on the floor around a geography book. It was his turn to flip the pages. As the pages were turned, everyone around the book would look for the word "Mississippi." The first person to find it and call out would win a point. When all the pages had been turned, the person with the highest number of points would win the game and become the designated page turner for the next round. Reggie came out of his dream at the point of handing over the book. When he first opened his eyes, he had the feeling his mother had just hugged him and assured him he was going to be alright. He looked out the window and saw that morning was breaking.

"Chicago. Next stop. We will be arriving in fifteen minutes," the conductor announced. Reggie's heart began to beat faster. He looked at Harry who turned his head from one side to another, but didn't open his eyes. Reggie reached over and shook his shoulder. Harry jumped as if he had touched an exposed nerve. He shook his head, wiped his eyes, and ran his fingers through his curly, brown hair.

"Fifteen minutes," Reggie told him.

"Ok, Ok, I'm ready. How are you doing?"

OK, Reggie said.

Nausea was rising in Reggie's stomach. "I'm doing good," he said. He stuck his hand underneath his sweater, pretending to adjust it and rubbed his upset stomach.

Harry pulled his duffle bag from the overhead rack, rested it on his lap and looked straight ahead as if waiting for the pistol to go off, signaling the beginning of the race. Reggie hoped he would find some place in the station where he could buy a cold Nehi orange drink to settle his stomach. Remembering he had not eaten since breakfast yesterday, he thought he was probably suffering from what folks often referred to as missed meal Colic.

When the train stopped, Harry bolted into the aisle and charged towards the nearest exit. Reggie tried to keep up, holding his suitcase close to his body to prevent it from striking anyone. They maneuvered their way through the crowd and finally landed on the sidewalk where they found a whole other crowd competing for taxis. One rolled up right beside them and Harry opened the door and jumped in. Reggie followed. As the taxi sped off, cold air hit Reggie in the face and almost knocked the wind out of him. He captured a deep breath and sat back in the taxi and began to take in Chicago.

Everything seemed bigger and faster than in Smoky Mountain and Danville, and there was more of everything. The tall massive buildings towering over the streets made each person walking beside them smaller. Reggie looked up, trying to count the stories of some of the buildings, but the taxi was moving too fast and it made him dizzy. Crowds jammed the sidewalks in what looked like well-rehearsed maneuvers. Reggie could not peel his eyes away from the streets. Stores, cafes, and apartments covered practically every space available. There seemed to be ten times more of everything in one block of Chicago than in the four blocks in downtown Smoky Mountain.

He had never seen so many cars and trucks move so slowly, except in a funeral procession. About three quarters of the people were white the rest were a mix of races.

The badge on the visor facing the driver read Ralph Polaski. His head seemed to be just above the dashboard. He drove with both hands gripping the steering wheel as he turned it from left to right dodging cars. He shouted, "Where did you get your driver's license, at the five and dime store?" Stopping at a traffic light, he looked in the rear view mirror and asked, "Are you guys coming home or visiting?"

"Both," Harry answered. "I'm home. My friend is visiting."

"Where are you from, young man?"

"Smoky Mountain, Tennessee, sir"

"Is that where they make that good bourbon whisky?"

"No sir. That's where they drink a lot of it."

The driver laughed. "Well, welcome to Chicago. It's probably a little noisier than Smoky Mountain, but a young man your age should enjoy the noise. Make sure you show him the Loop and Old Town."

"I will," Harry said.

The taxi driver wove expertly through the lanes. Every time Reggie felt they were about to land on the bumper of the car in front, he would swerve into the next lane or hit his brakes just in time. Reggie was so excited he forgot his nausea.

The taxi took a left turn and the sky opened up. Stretched out in front of them was that Great Lake, Lake Michigan, he had heard so much about. The waves in the blue waters hurled toward shore. He looked for the other side, but could not see it. It was the largest body of water he had ever seen. He couldn't imagine anyone swimming in it. The only body of water he had ever swum was the Orange Mound swimming pool on the other side of Smoky Mountain, the only public pool for Negroes. The pool started at three feet and rose to nine. He remembered how his friends dared him to jump off the diving board. It took them a week to convince him and after jumping he vowed to never do it again. It took too long to come to the surface. He and his friends would spend hot summer days there. He remembered how hungry they were at the end of a day in the pool. They would use their nickels to buy five oatmeal cookies and gulp them down as they rushed to the bus stop, hoping to avoid the neighborhood hoodlums who claimed Orange Mound was their turf and no one from outside could visit without answering to them. They usually asked no questions, just declared, "You are not from around here," and began chasing the intruders. They were especially on the look out on warm summer days when outsiders invaded the area. Reggie was from South Smoky Mountain which was also notorious for chasing out intruders. That made him and his crowd valued targets. It didn't matter they were not part of the gang of hoodlums in South Smoky Mountain.

Reggie sat up in his seat when he noticed the apartment buildings facing the lake. It was an awesome sight. What would it be like living in one of those apartments at the top of one of those buildings and facing a huge body of water? This must be the way rich people lived. In some ways, it was like living in a dormitory. Everybody had to be close to each other and there was no front or back yard. Neighbors could probably hear all the fuss going on in your house. Maybe you had to give up some privacy to live in a city as grand as Chicago.

After about a half hour, the taxi turned into the driveway leading to the entrance of a building facing the lake and Harry announced, "Well, here we are, home at last." Reggie was trying his hardest to not seem like some poor kid who had never left his county, but Harry could see the astonishment in his eyes. As the taxi driver took their luggage out of the trunk, a doorman came up to them, greeted Harry, picked up the luggage and carried them to the elevator.

The elevator made a quick journey to the tenth floor. Reggie and Harry stepped into the hall onto beautiful burgundy carpeting, which accentuated the white walls and crystal chandeliers hanging from the ceiling. Reggie, still trying to portray a person accustomed to such luxury, made no comment, but his face continued to give him away. As Harry opened the door, Reggie heard soothing music floating from the room to his right. The music seemed to beckon him to lose his troubles and come join a world of peace and serenity. He could not remember ever reacting to that kind of music before. It made him want to slow dance with Betty. The furniture he could see was a mixture of old and modern styles. The apartment had two wings and Reggie could see a panoramic view of the lake through the window facing him. An attractive woman emerged from the room with the music and rushed to Harry, giving him a hug and a kiss.

"I'm so glad you are home. You must be Reggie. It is indeed a pleasure to have you visit us for the holiday. I have heard so much about you. It seems I have known you for some time. My husband and I were so happy when Harry told us you had accepted our invitation."

"Thank you for inviting me. I'm really happy to be here," Reggie said as he tensed up to keep from exposing his awe.

"It is indeed our pleasure. You must be starving after the all night ride on the train. I'll tell Consuelo you are here and she will have some breakfast for you shortly. In the meantime, Harry, why don't you show Reggie to his room?" Mrs. Sanders looked as if she were in her twenties, but was obviously older. She had brown hair that reached her shoulders, large, soft brown eyes and skin color resembling someone from the southern Mediterranean. She was what Reggie had heard people describe as a classic beauty and was as warm as she was pretty. Her smile made him comfortable.

Harry led Reggie to his room and said, "You can unpack and relax. I will come and get you when breakfast is ready." Reggie could no longer maintain his cool when he stepped into his room.

"Man, this is nice," he said.

"Enjoy, I'll see you later," Harry smiled. The room had a view of the lake. The walls were beige with drapes to match. There was a large bed with a chocolate African design spread, a dresser that looked like it was built in another time, an old fashioned radio, a comfortable leather chair, two night stands holding shiny brass lamps, an oak desk and a valet at the foot of the bed. Reggie walked to the window and looked at the view. He could see the waves in the lake slapping the shore. He took a deep breath and picked-up that old suitcase that suddenly seemed more worn than he remembered and gingerly laid it on the bed and began to unpack.

17

THE TABLE WHERE THEY ATE BREAKFAST COULD HAVE EASILY SEAT TWENTY people. It stood on a thick red rug which matched the cushions on the chairs. There were two place mats at the far end of the table set for Reggie and Harry. Reggie took it all in without saying a word. Breakfast was Canadian bacon, scrambled eggs with onions, tomatoes and flavored with something Reggie could not place, English muffins, orange juice, strawberry jam and coffee. It looked like a good breakfast, but as hungry as he was, Reggie yearned for something that would stick to his ribs, like grits or rice. Mrs. Sanders joined them at the table and had a cup of coffee. "I am so pleased to have you with us. How are your parents?" Mrs. Sanders asked.

"They are fine," Reggie answered.

"What profession are you studying for?"

"I haven't given a profession much thought, but I imagine I will be a teacher," Reggie answered.

"That would be an honorable job that could be very rewarding. I bet your parents are proud of you," Mrs. Sanders said with a disarming smile.

"They are happy with the progress I am making," Reggie answered, thinking that his parents were not truly aware of his progress.

"I admire you for choosing a school that was recently integrated. It's the way to go, but true change doesn't come easy to some folks. I hope you are adjusting well," Mrs. Sanders said with a worried look. Reggie liked her. She had such a peaceful air and she seemed so genuine; however, he was not about to tell all of what he was experiencing at Davis to a white person. In this house he would hold tightly to those truths.

After breakfast, Harry announced that he needed a short nap and then he would be ready to tour the town. Reggie readily agreed. When he returned to his room, he turned on the radio and began searching for that station with the soft music that greeted him upon arrival. When he heard a violin, he realized he had found it. While it played a song that sounded like the beginning of morning, he decided to lay across the bed until Harry came for him. He could feel his heart beat slowing down and his muscles relaxing. The next thing he knew, Harry was shaking his shoulder.

"Is it time to go?" Reggie asked.

"Its six o'clock. Time to get ready for dinner. We are going out, so get ready and then come and meet my stepfather."

"Why did you let me sleep so long?" Reggie asked.

"I looked in on you a couple of times and called your name but there was no response, so I decided you needed the sleep. As a matter of fact, I went back to sleep each time after checking on you. So don't worry, we still have time to roam the city. You will get to see the city lights tonight when we go out to dinner." Harry assured him.

Reggie pulled out a pair of his tailor made pants and a matching sweater and declared he was ready to face the town. He walked out of his room and started towards the sound of voices. Suddenly, he was distracted by a man coming out of one of the bedrooms in the other wing of the apartment. Reggie immediately concluded that must be Harry's stepfather. There was something strangely familiar about him. "No way," Reggie mumbled to himself. He was dressed in what looked like an expensive navy blue suit with a white shirt and blue and red striped tie. His complexion was a couple of shades darker than Mrs. Sanders. He had straight black hair pulled back from his forehead. His lips were thin and his nose was medium sized. Without a smile, he extended his hand to Reggie and said, "I'm Nathanial Sanders and you must be Reggie Morton, welcome to our home. I hope you are comfortable. Let us know if we can do anything to make your stay as pleasant as possible. What did you do your first day in Chicago?"

"I am sorry to say sir I spent most of it sleeping," Reggie answered.

"Well, don't feel bad, your body was probably on overload and decided to break down so it could recharge. Let's find out if the other two are ready to go to dinner." Mr. Sanders said.

Mrs. Sanders looked at Reggie and Mr. Sanders with a big smile as they entered the room and said, "I see you have met Reggie."

"Yes I have and I see you two are ready, so let's be on our way."

As he waited with the Sanders family for the valet to bring the car, Reggie felt a hint of the mean Chicago winter. The cold winds he had heard so much about charged in from the lake, forcing him to struggle to maintain balance and protect his exposed face. Mr. Sanders stood stoically against the chill. He repeatedly turned his head in the direction of the garage and bit his bottom lip. Reggie kept mumbling to himself, "What I'm thinking can't be true."

Mrs. Sanders hugged her long fur coat and pulled the collar up to cover her neck and ears while her hair floated in the air. She leaned close to her husband, locked her arms around his and buried her head in his shoulder. It seemed she was searching for a sign of affection. He turned slightly, acknowledging her touch but quickly turned back in the direction of the garage. Harry stood behind his mother with his hands in his pockets looking at her and then back at his stepfather and nodded in approval.

Reggie stared at the family. When he thought one of them was about to turn in his direction, he quickly looked towards the lake. He was beginning to feel relaxed. He wanted to go up and give Mrs. Sanders a hug. She reminded him of Mona: beautiful, delicate, understanding and unafraid to show vulnerability. He thought she might be someone he could trust.

The temperature seemed to be dropping and Reggie wished he had those long johns he left behind. He paced back and forth to keep from shivering until he heard the sound of a motor. My God, is this their car?

When it stopped Mr. Sanders opened the door for Mrs. Sanders and charged to the driver's side where the valet, a dark skinned Negro who was whistling and popping his fingers ambled out. Mr. Sanders again bit his bottom lip, handed the valet a tip without making eye contact, then looked away as if he wanted to shower the valet with obscenities.

"What time did you say the reservation was for?" He asked Mrs. Sanders.

"Seven-thirty, dear, we should have time."

The car screeched out onto the street and off they sped in this black Mustang with red leather interior and a wood panel dashboard. Mr. Sanders twisted around until he found the position that seemed most comfortable. He gripped the steering wheel and seemed to move in rhythm with a cool jazz beat. He looked like a child enjoying a favorite toy. Mrs. Sanders clutched her purse tightly against her waist and bristled each time the car came to a sudden stop. She reached over with a shaking hand and touched her husband's arm. Mr. Sanders would turn, flashing a loving smile. She exhaled and her shoulders slumped for a moment, then he sped up again.

Reggie sat quietly taking it all in. His hands kept brushing the soft leather seat. His eyes trailed to the ceiling. It was fabric. This is a convertible. He smiled. He had never been in a Mustang before, but had dreamed of owning one. It was considered the coolest car on the streets these days, on the same level as the Cadillac, but more hip, especially a convertible. It was nothing like the old Mercury his father owned that always seem to need some repair. He and Doug swore when they were able to buy a car it would not be a Mercury. Reggie thought that maybe after landing a high paying job after college he would return home in a Mustang convertible and drive down Lauderdale Street tooting his horn. Every girl in the neighborhood would be checking him out, while Doug stood watching, jealous as hell.

As the car stopped, Reggie noticed the long stretched awning covering the path from the street to the restaurant entrance. It reminded him of the Gay Hawk Supper club on Orleans Street in Smoky Mountain where Negroes gathered on Saturday night and danced until dawn. As a young boy he used to stand in front of the Daise Theater across from the club and watch with wishful eyes, hoping for the day he would be allowed to enter. His father loved that place. His mother did too, though she refused to admit it. Going to night clubs was not something a good Christian spoke openly about.

"The name is Sanders," Mr. Sanders announced as he approached the maitre'di.

"Right this way, sir, your table is ready." The maitre'di led them to a table near a window with long purple velvet drapes.

"Your waiter this evening is John. He will be with you in a minute." He handed each of them a menu the size of a legal pad. The tables were covered with a white cloth and a candle burned in the center. Before each leather-cushioned chair were shining silverware and crystal, surrounding a white linen napkin. Waiters dressed in white jackets, black trousers, and black bow ties traversed the floor briskly. Reggie almost blurted out, "What a cool place," but he quickly regrouped and remembered he was trying to portray someone who was used to classy places.

Mr. and Mrs. Sanders were casually perusing the menu. Harry shuffled around in his chair. He kept turning his head from side to side and tracing his fingers over the menu as if he was looking for some familiar dish. John arrived, introduced himself and asked if they were having drinks before dinner. Mr. Sanders ordered a gin and tonic and Mrs. Sanders a white wine. Harry threw a quizzical glance at his mother. She offered no response. He ordered a coke. Reggie took Harry's cue and ordered the same. They all turned their attention back to the menu. There was so much on it that Reggie became confused. He had never heard of Chicken a la Champagne, Chicken Kiev or Chicken Fricassee and there was nothing that sounded like fried fish. He had been thinking about some crispy fried chicken since smelling it on the train. A couple of chicken legs, some potato salad, collard greens and hot cornbread would suit him well right now. Maybe that Chicken La Champagne will work, he thought, until he spotted the section for steaks. Steak was familiar but seldom found in his house so he decided on a T-Bone. Once the decision was made, he was able to focus on the ten dollar price. Back in Smoky Mountain, ten dollars was enough to feed his whole family for a couple of days. He wondered what they did to the beef to make it cost so much. He was almost embarrassed to order.

There was only one Negro couple in the whole place. Reggie was not sure whether he should be honored or scared. No one seemed to be bothered by him being there, but every now and then he felt a stare in his direction. Maybe they would think he was someone famous, like Sam Cooke, and whisper his name to each other. Someone might come by and ask for his autograph and he would politely say, sorry, I'm Reggie Morton of Smoky Mountain, Tennessee. He would love to tell that story to his friends.

As they waited for their drinks, Mr. Sanders decided it was up to him to break the silence. He surveyed the restaurant, nodded his head in approval, leaned back in his chair, positioning his hands on the arm rest, looked directly at Reggie and said with the authoritarian tone of a judge asking a criminal if he was going to commit another crime.

"What do you plan to do after college, young man?" The question caught Reggie off guard, but he felt ready for it. He had practiced earlier with Mrs. Sanders. He looked up from the menu and proudly announced, "I plan to be a teacher."

Mr. Sanders frowned. Reggie wanted to slide down in his chair until Mr. Sanders could no longer see him. He glanced over at Harry. Harry squirmed in his chair and looked everywhere except at Reggie, his mother, or his stepfather. This made Reggie feel even more anxious. He wondered if he was about to experience something Harry forgot to tell him.

"Why did you choose teaching?"

"It is a good paying job," Reggie said with a crack in his voice.

"Well, if you are looking for a good paying job, there are a lot out there that pay more than teaching. Have you considered law, medicine, engineering, business? They all pay more than teaching." Reggie's hands began to sweat. He felt his veil of cool and calm being torn away.

"No, sir, I have not considered those professions," he said with a slight lump rising in his throat.

"Well, you should. You have chosen a school where you can get a good education. You must take advantage of this opportunity. Teaching has been a traditional profession of Negroes for years because they accepted that as their limit. They don't usually venture out to pursue other professions because they accept their perception of limitation. Negroes tend to huddle in the security of their communities. Your choice of a college has sent you on a new path. You have to shed that perception." His voice lowered and he looked around the restaurant and continued. "I understand you are a very bright young man. You must use your intelligence and connections to the right people to expand your horizons, which I am sure go beyond the classroom." His eyes returned to meet Reggie's and, with what seemed like a pleasant look said, "When you finish school, you must come to Chicago where we can help to put you on the right track." He reached over and patted Reggie on the shoulder.

When Harry saw the pat, he plunged into the conversation with a swarm of words to rescue Reggie."Did you know the Panthers have gone undefeated in eight games? Coach Williams has the reputation of being one of the best in college football. Jerry Bryant, this year's quarterback, is talked about as a contender for the Heisman Trophy. You should see the crowd during the Saturday afternoon games. They come from all over the city to watch."

Mr. Sanders was looking away at people entering the restaurant. He immediately turned back and looked directly at Harry as if he were hearing him for the first time.

"Yes, oh yes, I have been following the Panthers ever since you enrolled at Davis. Bryant definitely has the potential to be in the pros and I sure hope the Bears are in a position and smart enough to get him. Do you think the Panthers might be a contender for the Cotton Bowl?"

"We are all hoping," Harry said. He leaned back in his chair proud of himself when he saw the tension subside in Reggie's face and the lines in his stepfather's disappear.

Reggie exhaled. He was glad Harry had taken the spotlight off him. But he was still trying to figure out if he had been put down, praised, chastised or what. He thought maybe the pat said, "I am not just criticizing, I care." However, Mr. Sanders seemed angry up to that point. It was hard to sum up this guy. The thought that something about him was familiar kept tugging at Reggie. I could be wrong, he thought.

For the past five minutes, Mrs. Sanders had been adjusting her wedding band and nervously casting her eyes between Reggie and her husband. She was concerned about what Reggie might be feeling; but she was also curious about her husband. She had never seen him interact with someone like Reggie.

"Do you have any sisters or brothers?" Mrs. Sanders asked Reggie, hoping to release the stress she perceived he had just endures.

"I have one brother. He is in the Army."

"Is he stationed overseas?"

"He's in South Carolina."

"I pray that he remains in South Carolina and not be sent to be on the front line of a war. It must be hard on your parents realizing that he could be sent to fight. What do your parents do?"

"My father works in a factory. My mother raised us kids."

"Have you spoken to your parents since you arrived?"

"No, I haven't"

"You must call them. They will be worried about you."

Reggie's mind began to race. I should have called as soon as I arrived, he thought. Mom will be pacing the floor and asking dad if he thinks I am all right. She'll be listening to the radio to hear if a train had an accident and jumping every time the phone rings. Before she goes to bed she will ask the Lord to take care of me and bring me back home safely. I sure hope the Lord tells her that I am okay and lets me know he's talked to her so both of us can sleep tonight.

"I will call in the morning. I don't want to wake them." Reggie said as calmly as he could.

"Don't forget," Mrs. Sanders said. She leaned back in her chair with a slight smile satisfied that she had fulfilled her obligation to rescued Reggie.

The waiter arrived with the orders. Reggie felt like he could eat a horse, but would settle for that dark brown piece of cow he ordered. To his great satisfaction, it was big. He sawed his knife into it and watched as a stream of blood crept onto the plate. It had a slight resemblance to a loser in a Saturday night brawl. He was too embarrassed to reject the steak so he took a bite and discovered it was juicy and tasty and not half as bad as it looked. The French fries were perfect, the green beans were all right, but they didn't have any ham or potatoes in them. The salad was just some raw vegetables, but the cheesecake with strawberries was something he had never had before, and it was delicious.

18

Reggie felt energized. His belly was full for the first time since he left the dorm and his body was rewarding him. Harry decided to give him his first ride on the "El" train. He explained that it traveled on tracks above and below ground and moved fast between stations and would get you to your destination faster than any other mode of transportation in the city. He then led him to an underground station which gave Reggie a reason for pause. He could visualize above ground but underground escaped his imagination – that was the place where dead people rested and sewage flowed. However, as they descended the stairs and entered the station, the bright lights illuminating the waiting area calmed him He looked around at the people on the platform and found no faces exhibiting fear, just impatience as some cast their eyes down the dark tunnel in search of the next train. A bright light busted out of the darkness slinging the sound of steel clashing against steel, drowning out all other sounds.

In a few seconds the train charged into the station; came to a halt and the crowd clustered around the doors rushed out as soon as the sliding doors opened. The crowd on the platform left a narrow path for those exiting and then shoved each other as they rushed into the train. The seats faced each other. Some passengers read, others looked up at the advertisements on the wall overhead and others stared into space. Nobody was making eye contact. Harry sat with his legs crossed and rested his head on the window behind his seat and held onto a pole. Reggie looked out the window into the darkness thinking that these people have no manners.

You would think someone could have said, "Good Evening." As the train moved swiftly over the tracks devouring curves, diving underground and surfacing again, Reggie felt like he was on the roller coaster ride at the Mid South County Fair which opened one week for Negroes during the annual fall celebration. There were all kinds of rides. He especially liked the "Pippin," the roller coaster that crept up a steep track and just dropped down sending his stomach racing for a new resting place.

The train emerged from the dark tunnel into a brightly lit station and Harry said, "Let's get off here." Harry led the way out. Reggie looked up the staircase and concluded this was the closest he had ever come to Hell. But when he saw the bright lights and flashing neon signs coming from all directions as they reached the street, he felt quite the opposite. With all the people walking around, it seemed more like a Saturday night on Deal Street in Smoky Mountain than a Wednesday night in Chicago.

They walked the sidewalks with Harry pointing to movie theaters, bars, and shops selling just about everything Reggie could imagine. I could get used to this fast, Reggie was thinking. They stood in front of this bar and paused, looking at each other with big smiles. There was muzzled music sounding like the blues and loud voices emitting indiscernible speech bursting into the street.

"No way, I don't want your parents or mom blaming me for your one night stay in a Cook County jail. Why don't we continue this tour tomorrow?" Harry said while shaking his head and placing his arms around Reggie's shoulder.

"Okay, buddy, let's go," Reggie said feeling a burst of euphoria as he realized he was actually seeing this city he had heard so much about.

Reggie was awakened the next day by a knock on his door. Harry peeped in and told him to come to breakfast when he was ready. Reggie, half asleep, turned to face Harry and waved his hand. The warm comfortable bed and soft pillows enveloped him. He wanted to just lie there at least another hour and feel this protection from all the hostilities he had met since arriving at Davis, but he knew that would not work. When he arrived in the dining room, there was only Harry. His parents were still asleep so Consuelo served them. Harry gave Reggie the itinerary for the day. He would continue a tour of the city's highlights and return home by three o'clock when guests were due to arrive for Thanksgiving dinner.

After breakfast, Reggie called his parents. Mrs. Morton answered the phone. "Well, I was wondering if you were all right and praying to God you were. How are things?"

"Things are wonderful, mom. I will write you all about it when I get back to school," Reggie answered.

"Have you spoken to Ellie yet?"

"Not yet, but I will," he answered.

"Well, make sure you do," an audibly disappointed Mrs. Morton urged him.

Harry and Reggie then headed out for the tour. Reggie wanted to ask Harry about his stepfather, but didn't know how to go about it. He recalled Harry saying he was still getting adjusted to him since his recent marriage to his mother. Now that Reggie had met him and been subjected to his lecture, he became more curious. He wanted to get Harry's reaction to the conversation at dinner last night because Harry didn't seem too comfortable during the time his stepfather was talking about Negroes. But Reggie decided maybe he needed to wait for an appropriate opening to bring up that conversation.

Harry took Reggie to see Wrigley Field, a place he had heard so much about during the baseball games he and Doug used to listen to on the radio. They walked along the Chicago River which Reggie had not heard about. He was fascinated to see it snake through town. He never thought of a river in the middle of a city. He always associated a river with the Mississippi River which separated Memphis from Arkansas. Chicago was as exciting to Reggie as he had imagined, and Harry was the happiest he had ever seen him. Reggie's excitement was tempered by the cold winds and he was not unhappy when Harry checked his watch and realized that it was two-thirty and time to return home.

When they arrived back at the apartment Reggie noticed Mr. Sanders was wearing a pair of slacks and an open shirt so he saw no need to put on the tie and jacket he had brought along for the occasion. He went to his room, turned on the radio, and lay across the bed listening to the soft music. He stared out the window looking over the lake and, for a moment, the peace he felt that morning returned; but slowly his thoughts traveled to some of the things Mr. Sanders had said the night before. He wondered if he should be focusing on a profession as Mr. Sanders had insisted. Teaching was definitely what most college graduates in his community did. Why shouldn't he teach? What did Mr. Sanders mean by *knowing the right people*? Was that a substitute phrase for *white people*? Was it really true that Negroes huddle in their communities for security? He never thought of it that way. Well, that certainly did not apply to him since he had enrolled at Davis University. Was Mr. Sanders serious about him returning to Chicago after graduation and helping him advance a career? He had never been confronted with these kinds of questions. His thinking had not gone any further than going to an integrated school and getting the same education that white people got. Reggie shook his head vigorously from side to side trying to evict all those troubling thoughts and questions that were disturbing his earlier feeling of peace.

The sound of chatter increased from the direction of the living room. He realized that guests had arrived and he had better join them. When he entered the living room, Mrs. Sanders began to introduce him. There were two couples, Dr. and Mrs. Hunt both seemed to be in their fifties or early sixties, and Mr. and Mrs. Woods were a mixed couple in their forties. Dr. Hunt was medical director at a private hospital in the city and Mrs. Hunt was a vice president at the Coleman Foundation, a philanthropic organization with a heavy emphasis on limiting pollution. Mr. Woods, a Negro, was a manager in marketing and his wife was a speech therapist. Soon, a Mrs. Lyons arrived, assumed to be in her middle thirties, and her teenage daughter, Cecilia. It seemed Mrs. Lyons was a divorcee living off alimony from a wealthy husband. Reggie was greeted enthusiastically by everyone. Mr. Sanders served as bartender and took orders for drinks. Consuelo brought in a tray of hors d'oeuvres that included boiled shrimp which immediately caught Reggie's attention. He had not had any shrimp since his days working with the caterer, Mrs. Hall. He kept looking at them when he was being introduced and as soon as he got a chance, he inched towards the tray and sampled a few. The sauce he dipped them into tasted just like Mrs. Hall's. He was tempted to stand near the tray and devour them, but Harry helped to save him from that embarrassment. He came over to Reggie after attempting to talk to Cecilia, who seemed shy and afraid to stray away from her mother.

Consuelo announced dinner. Seating had been arranged and Reggie was seated between the Hunts. He had been hoping to be next to Mr. Woods. He was curious about the Negro who married the *forbidden fruit*. Maybe, he hoped, Mr. Wilson would do something or say something that would shed some light on what that was like. He seemed so cool. Reggie had heard about Negro men married to white women, but had never met any. His thoughts turned to his attraction to Betty, but quickly tried to think of something else. When the Hunts discovered Reggie was between them, they both hugged him and said, "We got the guest of honor," which left Reggie feeling a bit self-conscious. He was not sure what the title required of him. It was hard enough sitting around the table with these rich people and facing more forks, spoons and glasses than he needed to consume a dozen meals which caused him to be one step behind everyone using them.

"I hear you are one of the bright freshmen at Davis University and I would like to congratulate you," Dr. Hunt began. "That is a great opportunity for young, underprivileged Negro kids to free themselves from the ghettos where they grew up. It must have taken a lot of courage to enroll in a recently integrated school. You should be proud of yourself. You are now on the right track to make something out of yourself. My wife and I would like to offer any assistance we can to help you through Davis and maybe you can return to Chicago after you graduate and work here. We can be of great assistance if you make that choice. We hope you will consider it," Dr. Hunt said.

"I will sir." The conversation caused Reggie to lose his apprehension about sitting next to the Hunts. He concluded Dr. Hunt was all right, but he wasn't sure about that description of him as underprivileged. His family was not rich, but they had never gone hungry and they were never on welfare. Of course, they certainly do not live like these white folks if that was what he meant.

"How are things going for you at Davis?" Mrs. Hunt asked while giving Reggie a soft hug.

"I'm doing fine so far," Reggie said, but his focus was now on the enticing food traveling in his direction and no one had even said grace. The turkey was golden brown. Mr. Sanders asked for his choice of meat. He requested dark meat and Mr. Sanders gave him the whole leg. He was embarrassed, but happy. Next came the candied yams, then stuffing with pork sausage. Reggie was disappointed. He was expecting to find oysters in the stuffing. There were green beans, but this was Thanksgiving and you were supposed to have some collard greens, he was thinking. When he bit into the food he concluded everything deserved a "B+". There was pumpkin pie for dessert which Reggie mistook for sweet potato pie. It was not as good as the sweet potato pie, but he gave it a "B–".

19

Reggie woke up around seven-thirty the morning after Thanksgiving and remembered that Harry mentioned he had a dental appointment and would probably be gone when Reggie got up, but he would be back around noon. Reggie rolled out of bed, tiptoed over to the window, opened the drapes, jumped back into bed and lay there comfortably looking out over the lake, asking himself if this could be him some day. Hunger drove him out of the bed into the shower and trailing down the hall towards the smell of bacon. I guess I can handle one of Consuelo's skimpy breakfasts after yesterday's dinner, he was thinking. As he turned the corner into the dining room, much to his chagrin there sat Mr. Sanders alone reading the paper and sipping a cup of coffee. Dear God, what test will he give me this morning. Is eating breakfast one by one how white folks do it, Reggie wondered?

"Good morning Reggie, come in and tell Consuelo how you want your eggs. It's just the two of us. Harry went to the dentist and Catherine went shopping. She likes to get a head start on Christmas."

"Over hard, please." Reggie called to Consuelo.

"Did you get a good night's rest?" Mr. Sanders asked.

"Yes, sir, I did. Lying in that bed felt like I was in a cradle and my mother was singing me a lullaby." Mr. Sanders relaxed the muscles in his face just enough to let Reggie know he had heard something requiring an emotional response and said, "Maybe I should try it some time."

"I had a great time yesterday. That was some really good food. I hope I didn't embarrass you by eating as much as I did. Everything tasted so good, I couldn't help myself," Reggie confessed.

"We were happy you enjoyed it and the more you ate the more we were sure you did. Consuelo is a great cook. We were all once in college and understand how cafeteria food tastes."

"I think Doctor Hunt and his wife are nice people. I enjoyed talking to them," Reggie said with glowing eyes.

"Yes, they are. We are lucky to have friends like them. I really like Chicago and the people I have met since coming here. This is a good place to live, work and meet interesting people. I'm not saying we don't have our problems like any other city. Those hoodlums in the street gangs hurt our image. If I had my way I would hang every one of them by their necks. The only goal they seem to have in life is crime and dependency. There is far too much time spent by those so called civil rights groups trying to elevate the lives of people who have no desire to go anywhere other than where they are. And then there are the self-designated civil rights leaders who seem to be motivated by self-aggrandizement to prove their manhood. They hold the rest of us hostage to an elusive principle of equality for all. There is no such thing and we need to face it and do whatever it takes to protect ourselves from those hoodlums. As I have said many times, Negroes need to shed the bondage of their past and embrace the present just as you have by choosing to go to an integrated school where you will learn how the real world works."

He paused for a moment then said, "You have to excuse me Reggie. I get angry and go off on a rant sometimes. I really admire what you are doing to liberate yourself from your community. A bright young man like you deserves to rise to the top and I would like to do whatever I can to help you get there. Listen, enjoy your breakfast and make yourself comfortable, I am off to a game of tennis. Harry said he will be back around noon."

Mr. Sanders left Reggie trying to sift through his second lecture. Maybe he likes me, but not many other Negroes.

"I will see you later," Mr. Sanders called out as he left the apartment.

"Over hard?" Consuelo asked as she sat down a plate of eggs, bacon and toast.

"That's right," Reggie said as Consuelo disappeared into the kitchen and reappeared with a cup of coffee heavy with cream and boldly sat across the table from him.

"Thanks for the fantastic Thanksgiving dinner. I hope we are having leftovers today. I can't wait for some more of those candied yams and that turkey," Reggie said.

"Well, thank you, I am glad you enjoyed my cooking; but I can't take credit for the yams. Those were done by Mr. Sanders. He used a recipe he says has been in his family for many years. I hear you can get some really good food in New Orleans."

"Is that where Mr. Sanders is from?" Reggie asked.

"Oh, yes, I think he still has family there, but he doesn't seem to visit them." Consuelo sat down her cup of coffee, looked across the table at Reggie, lowered her voice just above a whisper and said, "One day when I was cleaning their bedroom, I saw a picture of an elderly couple. Mrs. Sanders said they were Mr. Sanders' parents. The woman had long grey hair a light skin complexion and the man had skin the color of Mr. Sanders and short cropped straight hair. "He looked like a Negro to me," Consuelo said. As soon as the word 'Negro' escaped Consuelo's mouth, Reggie's felt like he had been given a shot of corn whiskey. He immediately decided his thoughts were right about Mr. Sanders. He put down his fork and began to wonder if he had slipped and said something out of order that may have offended Mr. Sanders. He tried to remember all the things Mr. Sanders had talked about and tried to make sense of them now that he suspected he was a Negro. Coming from New Orleans, Reggie wondered if he was one of those *passing* Negroes. He didn't want to start probing Consuelo. He was not sure he could trust her. Maybe he would ask Harry, but if Mr. Sanders was passing, Harry would not know and the question could really shake him up.

Reggie sat in dumbfounded silence while Consuelo continued to talk. He did not want to interrupt because she might answer his questions without being asked. She seemed to have an audience she had never had before so the gossip and rumors she had not been able to share with anyone who might appreciate hearing them from her poured out.

"I heard his mother's grandfather was actually white. His sister visited him once and she looked just like any white woman on the streets. I believe he has known the Hunts for a long time. They introduced him to Mrs. Sanders. He was working as a lawyer for the city, his first job after graduating from the University of Chicago Law School.

"Mrs. Sanders got him the job at the big law firm where he works now and they were married and he moved in before we knew it. I don't mean he is a bad man. Mrs. Sanders is the happiest I've ever seen her since they've been together. The poor child has had some hard times in her life. Her father owned a big company and they were tough parents and they did not approve of her marriage to Harry's father. He made furniture from scratch. He was so handsome and charming, but not very rich. Mrs. Sanders was always arguing with her father before he and her mother were killed in an automobile accident. She was their only child and with her inheritance she has no money problems. After her husband died, she clung to Harry."

"You must have known the Sanders for a long time?" Reggie asked.

"I worked for her parents and have been here since they died. Have you and Harry been friends that long?"

"I met him at the beginning of the school year." Reggie said.

"I was wondering because he's never brought around any Negroes before. Well, your being here has really made Mrs. Sanders happy."

"Where did you hear Mr. Sanders great grandfather was white?" Reggie asked.

"I talk to people", Consuela said as she smiled and winked. Harry breezed into the dining room. "Its time to give Chicago a final sweep before returning to school," he announced. Consuelo dodged into the kitchen like a mouse when a light comes on. The rest of the day Reggie and Harry spent meeting old friends of Harry's. A light-skinned black face would occasionally appear among the crowd. Each looked like they could be a brother or sister of Mona's. That evening Harry took Reggie to a house party. He proudly introduced him to the host and guests, all white. Reggie was very popular with the girls. Different ones came over and asked him to dance. He felt comfortable as long as the music was for fast dancing; but when it slowed down and you were expected to hold your partner close, he felt nervous. There were dagger stares from some of the boys. Harry kept coming over to Reggie and placing his hand on Reggie's shoulder and asking, "How are you doing, buddy?"

"I'm good," Reggie would say.

When Harry came to awaken him at seven o'clock Saturday morning, Reggie realized there were only twelve hours before the train back to school. He felt sad that the weekend was coming to an end. He had seen how some white folks do some things and he was pleased with what he saw. But he doubted he could ever have what they had in spite of what the Hunts and Mr. Sanders said. He certainly did not have the complexion to pass, if that was what Mr. Sanders was doing. But maybe they could help him get the kind of job where he could earn enough money to rent a nice apartment in Chicago. "Boy, have I got a lot to tell people back in Smoky Mountain when I get home for Christmas," he thought.

Most of Saturday was spent tagging along with Harry and Mrs. Sanders as they attended to priorities set by Mrs. Sanders, shopping for Harry, visiting Harry's father's grave and leaving flowers, helping Harry pick his Christmas present for Mr. Sanders. Reggie dreamed of spending money the way they were as he continued to see all the beautiful things he wanted to buy for his mother and Mona. One of the department stores was twice the size of Goldblaths in Smoky Mountain and had the escalator Reggie had never seen. It was as much fun riding the escalator as it was watching those rich people spend money.

After a dinner of lobster, potatoes au gratin, steamed vegetables, green salad and apple pie, Reggie felt he had a meal that might stick to his bones. He returned to his room, closed the door and stood in silence. He wanted to lie down in that bed one more time and take a nap, but there was no time. Harry charged into his room to gather his bag. Mrs. Sanders hugged Reggie and told him how much they enjoyed his visit and how they looked forward to his next trip. She handed him an LP with a long list of classical tunes, including "Morning" from the Peer Gwent Suite, the music he heard when he arrived. Reggie was surprised she had noticed and thanked her over and over again. Mr. Sanders shook Reggie's hand and told him to work hard at Davis and it would pay off. He reminded Reggie he had friends in Chicago that cared about his well-being and he should always keep that in mind. Consuelo emerged from the kitchen and said in a formal but friendly way that it had been a pleasure meeting him and then when she was sure that no one was looking, she winked and smiled.

Harry returned and hugged his mother, shook his stepfather's hand, hesitated for a moment, then gave him a quick hug. He hugged Consuelo and he and Reggie bolted out to take the last trip on the El train to the station.

Reggie led the way when the call came for their train to board and marched into a car where he saw a few white passengers. Harry didn't seem to notice. He hadn't stopped talking since leaving the apartment about what a great Thanksgiving he had. "Thanks Reggie," he said.

"I should be thanking you. What did I do to deserve your thanks?" For the first time since they left the apartment, Harry went silent. He looked at Reggie as if he was seeing him for the first time.

"Well everyone liked you."

"I liked them too and I'm really glad you invited me. This was the best time I've ever had." Harry took Reggie's hand in both of his, shook it and said, "I'm glad. I'm glad. I think my stepfather and I are going to get along really well now and that would make mom happy." Reggie was curious what Harry meant by the statement, but he wasn't comfortable pursuing the subject. He was feeling too good about the trip and did not want to feel that he had been used.

Reggie lay back in his seat, thinking about how his dream of going to Chicago had come true and exceeded all expectations. He began to feel good about Mr. Sanders pushing him to think of options after graduation. He was proud that everyone believed he was smart and had a promising future as a result of his having gone to Davis. He thought maybe this is the way white folks treat you when they like you. It seemed to have worked for Mr. Sanders, but he wondered if Negroes helped by rich white people wound up disliking other Negroes the way Mr. Sanders seemed to.

20

Upon arriving back in the dorm, Reggie headed straight for the mail box. He was not disappointed. There was a letter from Mona. He couldn't wait to get upstairs to read it. He had already planned to write and tell her about his trip before going to bed. After dropping his bags and taking off his coat, he fell on the bed and ripped open the letter. It began with the usual greeting,

"My dear Reggie," and went on to say, "my dream of seeing you at Christmas has just been shattered. My parents called and said we are going to celebrate Christmas in Birmingham with my grandmother because she has not been well and my father wants to spend the time with her because we may not have her with us for another Christmas. We will be there until after the New Year so when I leave I will have to go directly back to school. I have been crying ever since I got their call. Do you know whether you will be able to come home during the Easter break? I really looked forward to seeing you."

Reggie dropped the letter to the floor, placed his hands behind his head and stared at the ceiling. He thought of something his mother often said: "When God closes a door he opens a window." He looked around and found both of his windows were closed. The hurt he felt churned his stomach but he could not cry. He wanted to hit something, break something or spew a litany of profanity. He stood up and paced the room hitting his fist into his hand. He decided he had to get out of the room so he went for a walk. The campus was relativity quiet. Every now and then a car unloaded a student with bags over their shoulders and under their arms. It was a very cool fall day, but the sky was clear and the sun was shining brightly. Reggie was walking without a conscious destination as his mind worked to heal his pain. Before he realized where he was going, he had wandered back into the campus garden. The trees had shed most of their leaves and the shrubbery had turned brown, but the bright sun and serenity gave the place a lasting beauty. Reggie found the same bench where he had cried months ago. He wondered if Dr. Townsend had cooked up the plot about the grandmother's illness just to keep Mona from seeing him. He thought how great it would be to show up in Birmingham and see the look on their faces. As he sat there anger turned to fear. The longer they were apart, the greater the chance she would stop loving him. He always feared she would meet other men in New York who would pursue her. Now he felt he was going to lose her and there was nothing he could do about it.

Then there was the problem of responding to her letter. Could he tell her things would eventually work out if they stayed determined? Could he express sympathy for her grandmother when he thought the whole thing was just a plot cooked up by her father.

He picked himself up off the bench and began the walk back to the dorm. When he entered his room, he suddenly remembered the record Mrs. Sanders had given him. He took it out of the jacket, placed it on the turntable and switched it on. The first tune was Debussy's Clair De Lune. As the music flowed through the room and he began to unpack, those clouds of doubt seemed to slowly dissipate. He decided he could write Mona. He would assure her his love would last far beyond Christmas and Easter and that her ailing grandmother deserves to have her family around at a time like Christmas. He told her he was disappointed, but they would make up for it at Easter and during the summer. He went on to describe his trip to Chicago and the really nice people he met there.

21

THE DISTANCE BETWEEN THANKSGIVING AND CHRISTMAS SEEMED TO BE measured in inches as Reggie plowed through the number of papers due before the Christmas break. During those few weeks, most of his time was spent in the library and at the desk in his room. Studying had taken on new meaning after the trip to Chicago. He became determined to defeat Professors Schulman and Woodcliff. He turned in his last paper the day before classes ended. That night he stuffed his clothes in his old suitcase and early the next morning he was off to the Greyhound station, heading for home.

It seemed like ages since the day he arrived at the station all eager and curious. He certainly felt like a different person. After finding a seat on the bus and storing away his suitcase overhead, Reggie leaned back in his seat and closed his eyes. He slept deeply until the bus arrived in Smoky Mountain. One of the city's tank sized sanitation trucks slowly moved down Main Street releasing powerful spews of water that pushed all the debris in its path into the gutters. He noticed the whites-only Grand Old Winsor Hotel still had the tall, dark-skinned Negro in that grandiose uniform greeting guests.

Reggie took the Number Thirteen bus from the station. It snaked through the familiar streets and finally entered South Smoky Mountain. There was Long Hardware with the same old Christmas wreath on the door and the wooden reindeer perched on each side. Rexall Drug's store window was filled with red and green streamers, empty boxes wrapped in colorful Christmas paper and a statue of dear old Santa with his pack on his back standing in the center of the gifts. The Holly trees along Simpson Street were bursting with ripe red berries. Steam crawled from the back windows of Fargo Cleaners. Everything looked the same, but different. It was a curious feeling, but the thought of seeing his family and friends excited Reggie, even though Mona's absence made him sad.

Mrs. Morton was looking out the window when he entered the yard. She rushed to meet him and gave him a hug and a kiss. "Son, it is so good to see you and have you home. Come on in here and let me fix you some breakfast. Doug is on furlough and will be here tomorrow. I just don't know what I am going to do with myself. Both of my boys home for Christmas."

"It's really good to be home. They have been working me like a hound dog and it is great to get away from that place for a while. Do I smell biscuits? Well, if I do, all you have to do is throw in a couple of slices of bacon and bowl of grits and I am your happy son."

"Go on back there and put your things down and put your dirty clothes in the hamper. By that time your breakfast order will be ready." Reggie walked into his room. It seemed small and a bit crowded. He fell down on his bed, looking for that familiar comfort. For a minute he found it, but in a short time a feeling of sadness crept in.

His mother was all smiles as Reggie came into the kitchen for breakfast. "Now you sit down and eat all you want. I know you haven't had any good food like this in a long time. I want you to enjoy it while you are here. You never did get around to telling me about the trip to Chicago. How was it? Did you ever see Ellie Mae?"

"Mom! I had the time of my life. The Sanders live in an apartment facing Lake Michigan. They have a maid. They took me to an expensive restaurant and I had a big steak and cheesecake. I had my own room with a view of the Lake. I met their friends. They all liked me and want to help me get a job when I finish college. I'm pretty sure Mr. Sanders is a light-skinned Negro who could pass for white. He is a lawyer in a big law firm in Chicago. Mrs. Sanders comes from a very rich family. They invited me back for a visit and I would like to go. We went all over the city. There is so much activity there and people crowd the streets they way we do at the Cotton Carnival. I really think that I want to live there when I graduate."

"I can see you really had a good time," Mrs. Morton said. "Well, I guess with all that education you are getting, you might think you are outgrowing Smoky Mountain. I'm goanna have to take that to the Lord and ask his guidance. I guess you didn't see Ellie Mae."

"No, mom, I didn't have enough time. Maybe the next time I am there I will look her up."

"You have to find time," she scolded him. "Ellie Mae will be upset to think that you were there and didn't even say hello. Tell me about your grades and your teachers," Mrs. Morton asked, taking a breath. Reggie hesitated then continued to chew his food and describe Davis' beautiful campus and garden. He then told her he had some tough teachers and he had to get used to their standards; however, he was doing his best. He warned her it was hard to excel in every subject in college.

"Tell me about that teacher who gave you the tickets to that play."

"Dr. Thorn is really a very nice lady. She used to teach at LeMoyne College in Memphis so I think she understands a lot about Negroes. She told me to work hard and things would go well for me at Davis."

In the middle of their conversation, they heard what sounded like movement in the front room. Mrs. Morton looked curiously at Reggie. Reggie stood up and before he could move a voice yelled out, "Anybody home?"

"Oh, my Lord, it's Douglas!" Mrs. Morton shouted. By that time Doug had entered the kitchen. He dropped his duffel bag and wrapped his arms around his mother and they both were brought to tears. As their hug was broken, Mrs. Morton said, "I wasn't expecting you until tomorrow."

Doug explained that he was able to leave a day early and got a ride with another soldier all the way to Smoky Mountain. "Well, look who is stuffing his face, Joe College. Are we still able to communicate or have you gotten too highly educated to deal with your under educated brother?" Doug asked. Reggie leaped up grinning and grabbed Doug's hand with both of his as Mrs. Morton released Doug from her grip.

"Welcome home soldier. Don't worry, I will always be able to communicate with you. After all, education teaches you to communicate with all people and that includes you," Reggie smiled. They both let out a hearty laugh from their stomachs.

Mrs. Morton immediately prepared a plate for Doug and the three sat around the table for hours talking about the mischief Doug used to get into and the whippings he got and how Reggie always looked for ways to make money so he could buy things his parents couldn't afford. Mrs. Morton kept touching each of them. "Now you two must get out of my kitchen so I can prepare a celebration dinner," Mrs. Morton ordered.

Reggie and Doug went to their room. As soon as the door closed behind them, Doug asked Reggie, "Have you had a taste of the forbidden fruit yet?" The question caught Reggie off guard. He immediately visualized Betty, which stirred fear and desire in him at the same time.

"No, brother, I have not dived into the forbidden fruit bowl. At Davis forbidden fruit really means forbidden. A Negro boy was dating a white girl at the beginning of the semester and the school sent her, and not him, home. What do you think of that? I don't plan to let the forbidden fruit ruin my chance to get my degree." He didn't want to tell Doug about Betty because Doug would have urged him to pursue the relationship and he was set on doing just the opposite. It got him thinking though, and he realized he had better decide what he intended to leave out of his accounts of life at Davis when speaking to people. He did not want to reveal his disappointments. He felt anxious to move the conversation away from him.

"Those are unusual white folks at your school," Doug declared. "In that case, I can't depend on you to give me the goods on college-educated white chicks."

"That's right," Reggie said. "What is it like in the Army? What do they do to make you a killer?"

"All soldiers are not in infantry, my brother. There are many jobs to be done for Uncle Sam. I work behind a desk."

"How did you get those three stripes on your arm?" asked Reggie.

"Those stripes tell you that I am not just any soldier. I am a sergeant. I'm moving up in the ranks with a lot of soldiers below me."

"Well, what about your escapades? Have you received the reward of any fruit, yet?"

"My, brother, this uniform and those three stripes give me a pass into the bedrooms of many foxy mamas. And now that I am home for a few days, I need to dust off my old black book and let the flock know I am in town and watch them racing to get under this uniform." He pulled his small black notebook out of his pocket and checked off some numbers and went for the telephone. He kept dialing until he scored. "Well, brother, I'm all set for the evening; how about you?"

"How would I know? You've held up the phone all this time to make your hit. I haven't had a chance to call anybody. It looks like your uniform has lost some of its magic in Smoky Mountain. It took so long for you to get a yes."

"Never mind me, let me see what you can do. The phone is all yours," Doug said.

Around four-thirty the old Mercury pulled up in front of the house and Mr. Morton rolled out in his usual deliberate pace. Reggie saw him first and said to Doug, "Let's stand in front of the door so when he opens it, he will look straight into our eyes." Mr. Morton took his time getting to the door and it seemed like his mind was a million miles away. When he opened it and saw his two sons, his eyes bucked and he said, "What the hell." He dropped the bag he was carrying and reached out to shake their hands. Doug gave him a solid handshake. Reggie's was not as solid, but he used both hands.

"When did you two get here? Well, I'll be damned. Your mother must be thinking the good Lord came down just to hand her a blessing and I can tell from the smells coming out of the kitchen she plans to make this day one to remember." This was more animation than either of the boys had ever seen coming from their father.

"Dinner will be ready as soon as Roy has had a chance to wash up," Mrs. Morton proudly announced. As the family took their seats around the table, a flash of euphoria traveled through Mrs. Morton. She almost felt like shouting. The whole family was again together around the table as if life had not changed. They bowed their heads and she began, "Thank you God for bringing my sons home again safe and in good health and for blessing them with such great opportunities to make something out of themselves and we thank you for your many blessings and for this food we are about to eat. Amen." Everybody open their eyes to fried chicken, smothered cabbage with okra, black eyed peas, sliced tomatoes, corn bread, peach cobbler and iced tea. As usual, conversation died while the dinner was consumed. But as the main course was reaching the digestive stage and before the much anticipated peach cobbler was brought to the table, Mr. Morton broke the tradition by asking Doug how he made sergeant so fast.

"Didn't you know you had a smart son? I outsmarted my superiors along the way and became a natural for promotions each time I was eligible."

"Well, whatever that means, congratulations," Mr. Morton said.

Mrs. Morton looked across the table at Mr. Morton and smiled.

"I don't mind the service now. In the beginning I hated it. Everywhere you looked there was a white prejudiced superior officer who seemed to be from some police force that was used to beating up on Niggers. There were a lot of Negro soldiers in my unit and we stuck together. That helped us cope with the crackers. My rank is higher than many soldiers, white and Negro. I'm working in Material right now. I don't think I'll have to play cowboy on the front line of any war. The army ain't a bad deal."

"Thank God," Mrs. Morton said.

"What's it like for you at Davis son?" Mr. Morton asked Reggie.

"I am doing well in my classes. My grades are good now. We won't get grades that will be in our final record until late January after we complete final examinations. College is much harder than high school, but I'm coping with it." Reggie answered. A lump rose in his throat. He didn't want to lie or tell the whole truth.

What's it like being in a school forced to admit Negroes? How many other Negroes are there? Are there any Negro teachers on the faculty? Reggie felt like the room was getting warmer. He wanted to say to his father one question at a time, but knew he couldn't and still hide his discomfort.

"There's only a handful of Negro students enrolled and no Negroes on the faculty. I'm the only Negro in all my classes and sometimes I get stares from some of the other students when I speak. I have one professor who really likes me, and the guy I went to Chicago with at Thanksgiving is a real good friend."

"What about that trip to Chicago? Were those rich people you stayed with? How did they treat you?" His father asked. Reggie felt a shot of adrenalin invade his bloodstream. His eyeslids parted as if he had seen a ghost while a huge smile covered his face. He placed his elbows on the table and his hands began to move in harmony with his voice.

"Dad, that was a fantastic trip! Those people are rich and live in an apartment with more rooms than most houses I have been in. It faces Lake Michigan. I had my own room and it faced the Lake. They took me out to an expensive restaurant and showed me the town where people seemed to stay up all night doing things. They invited me back and said they wanted to help me get a job when I finish college. Mr. Sanders looks like a Negro who could pass for white. Mrs. Sanders is white and comes from a rich family. They have a Mexican maid. Mr. Sanders congratulated me for choosing to go to a great school like Davis. He said I was smart and brave. I think he likes me; but he has some bad opinions of Negroes. He said Negroes tend to stay huddled in their communities feeling safe among their own and are not willing to venture out in the real world. He seems to think too many Negroes are either criminals like the street gang members he wanted to hang by their necks or those satisfied to depend on the government for handouts. He said too much time is spent by so-called Civil Rights leaders trying to change the lives of people who are going nowhere and who are satisfied with where they are. He said most of those self-appointed leaders are just uneducated preachers trying to assert their masculinity and stroke their egos by taking charge of something they can control. What they need to be doing, he said, is helping Negroes put their past behind them and focus on the present. They need to know that a good education and knowing the right people is the way to get ahead. I told him I wanted to be a teacher when I graduated from Davis because it was a good paying job. He didn't like that. He said I probably made that decision because Negro college graduates have always gone into teaching which shows one of the downfalls of Negroes, accepting limitations. I met some of their friends and they liked me too. There was a Dr. Hunt. He also congratulated me for going to Davis. He agreed with Mr. Sanders that it would be helpful in getting a good job. He also suggested I return to Chicago after graduation where they could be in a position to help me get on the right track. They all really liked me. I think I want to be a lawyer like Mr. Sanders."

Reggie's enthusiasm left the family in awe. They were surprised he had not passed out since he was talking nonstop seemingly without taking a breath. They were glad they could take a break from trying to absorb everything he was saying.

Mrs. Morton was stunned he could be so excited after hearing all those things disrespecting Negro history. "I don't know Mr. Sanders," she said, "or your Dr. Hunt, but I guarantee you what they know about Negro history could fit in a bottle cap." Her jaws were tight, her teeth gripped together, and she spoke through her nose. "We are not huddled in our communities because we want to. They won't let us go any place else and who ever heard of forgetting the past. If we did that, we might start thinking like them and end up believing we don't deserve equal rights. What did he mean we accepted limitations? If that was true you would not be going to Davis today. The Negroes in Montgomery would still be riding in the back of the bus, and there would be no Jackie Robinson, Ralph Bunche or Marian Anderson. Mr. Sanders and Dr. Hunt need someone to beat some sense into them. Mr. Sanders must be one of those Negroes who wants to be something he ain't. He must have some screws missing in his head or maybe it's just filled with snort and water. May the good Lord bless him and the devil doesn't catch him. I don't know what kind of track your Dr. Hunt thinks he can put you on that you are not already on. He probably comes from a long line of carpetbaggers."

"Mom, don't get excited. These people really think I am smart and are probably in a position to help me achieve big success. I thought that would make you proud."

"Look here boy, I am proud of you for going after the same education white folks get, but I don't want you going off thinking Negroes can't do anything right or everything white folks do is right. I want you to get the best education you can, but I don't want you to lose your common sense. The Brown decision opened the door to opportunities. It doesn't mean we need to forget who we are or where we came from. If you start thinking like Mr. Sanders and your Dr. Hunt, white folks will chew you up and spit you out before you know what happened. That would break my heart."

"Okay, Mom, Okay, Mom, I hear you," Reggie responded but he really was not concentrating on what she was saying. His mind was clouded by her emotional reaction and he just wanted her speech to come to an end. Chicago had been the best thing that happened to him since leaving home to go to Davis.

Doug went out after dinner to chase his hit from the black book. Reggie remained in their room with the intention of studying. Alone however, his thoughts drifted back to his mother's angry reaction. He never dreamed she would react that way. God knows he did not want to disappoint his parents. But Dr. Hunt and Mr. Sanders were nothing like Drs. Schulman and Woodcliff or the guys at Omega Alpha. He felt lonely, but dismissed the feeling thinking the joy of being home for Christmas would return when he met his friends the next day.

Alone in their room, Mrs. Morton said to Mr. Morton, "That trip to Chicago seemed to have had a big impact on Reggie. I think he was willing to overlook the crazy ideas those folks had about Negroes. Has he forgotten everything we taught him that fast? He's only been gone four months"

"Well, you were all excited about the possibilities after the Brown decision and told the boy one day he would be able to compete with white folks. So what do you expect? The boy has seen enough prejudice to know you can't let your guards down. He should have enough sense to know we are not all lazy and useless," Mr. Morton said.

"Yes, but I wish there were some Negroes with their heads on straight at Davis that could influence him," Mrs. Morton protested.

"Well, he has to grow up sometime. We can't hold him under our wings forever." Mr. Morton responded.

"I know that," Mrs. Morton sighed with anger in her voice.

The first thing on Reggie's mind the next morning was seeing Arnold, Alfred and Beverly. It had all been arranged the day before that they would meet at Harlem House. When Reggie arrived, Mr. Snow greeted him with a strong, hearty handshake and asked how things had worked out at Davis.

"Just fine," Reggie said without hesitation. "My grades are good. I've met some nice people. I spent Thanksgiving in Chicago with one of my classmates. It was a great trip. I think I might go back there after I graduate."

"I'm really glad to hear that. I crossed my fingers everything would go well for you. I was afraid they would try everything they could to make it hard since they fought so long to keep Negroes out. Well, maybe those folks at Davis have finally come around to respecting the law. I had my doubts. Let me congratulate you young man. Keep up the good works. I know you will make us all proud." Reggie felt ashamed that he had not been completely open with Mr. Snow.

In walked Arnold, followed by Beverly and Alfred, "Look at Mr. Davis College in his blue jeans and Davis sweatshirt," Beverly said. "I guess that shows he is a true Davis man."

"Well, what have you got to say for yourself, Mr. Davis Man?" Alfred and Arnold tuned in. Reggie loved the sound of Davis Man. It reminded him of the things Mr. Sanders said about his decision to enroll there. That was how he wanted his friends to see him, so he said, "Well, what can I tell you? You're looking at a Davis College scholar." They all broke out in loud laughter, shook hands and embraced each other.

"Well, how are things at our elite Negro college in our nation's capital? Have you had your quota of fine chicks yet or does it take two semesters to reach your maximum?" Reggie asked Arnold.

"I'm working my way to the max in my own time. I know what's on the menu so I don't have to rush. I can take my time and enjoy each dish along the way," Arnold said as he pounded his chest.

Reggie lashed back, "That means he probably hasn't scored at all. Besides your low score, what about Howard?"

"It's full of 'siddity' Negroes, zebra professors and hungry, foxy chicks. Nothing I can't handle and that includes the siddity hungry chicks, contrary to your misguided assessment."

"Well, Beverly, have the snow and cold winds done anything to you other than make your skin ashy?" Arnold asked.

"The one good thing about Minnesota is it is far from foolish Negroes like you," Beverly snapped.

"Hey Alfred, what has it been like holding down Smoky Mountain since I left town? Were the women crying like lost lambs for me?" Arnold asked.

"I haven't had to wipe one tear from their eyes. There are some real foxy chicks over at Lane and they don't mind giving a dude some time. We have some tough professors there that hound you day in and day out about your studies and how to become great Negroes. In spite of my commitment to give the chicks equal time, I'm a real Lane scholar. I was sporting a 'B+' average at Mid Terms." Alfred said. "How about that?"

"Come on Beverly, tells us about life up North." Reggie asked.

"Well, I'm having the time of my life. So far I have only gotten one 'B' on an exam. The rest of my grades have been 'A's. I have some great professors. Everybody is friendly. There are about fifty Negroes out of two thousand students. Most of the Negroes come from out of state and live in the dormitories; however, my roommate is white and she comes from Seattle, but I have friends among the other Negroes. As you have been so anxious to point out, Minnesota is very cold in the winter but it is a beautiful state with all its lakes. The fall foliage is something to behold. You really need to see it."

Reggie was glad she spoke first about her experiences because, after hearing her story, he was more determined his bad times at Davis would remain his secret.

"Now, Mr. Integrations, tell us about Davis," Arnold asked. Reggie wanted to talk about his trip to Chicago, but realized his friends would not let him get away with that so he told them there were only a handful of Negroes enrolled and only one other lived in the dorm, but he had made friends with white students and as a matter of fact he had gone home to Chicago with one for the Thanksgiving break.

"Wow! what was that like?" Arnold asked with a sober look of surprise.

Reggie perked up and described the things he did and saw. He went on to describe the family that invited him and the different people he met. He talked about how everyone treated him and his desire to go back after he finishes college. He felt relieved. He had turned the conversation away from the whole story of his life at Davis.

Arnold put his hand on Reggie's shoulder and said, "Brother you had better watch yourself around all those white folks; you just might lose your soul." Reggie was so relieved he had diverted their attention away from life at Davis that Arnold's statement bounced right off of him.

"Hey man where is Mona?" Alfred asked. The question made Reggie feel like someone had touched an exposed nerve. He took a deep breath then gave them her story. The group looked at each other with a bit of mischief reflecting in their eyes.

"I'm sorry," Arnold began. "I hope her grandmother enjoys the visit, but I think Mona better watch you now that you are around all those pretty white girls looking to test the Negro male mystique," Arnold said with less than a full smile.

"Mona has nothing to worry about," Reggie shot back.

"If you say so," the groups said in unison and then burst out laughing. Reggie was irritated, but managed to force a smile as the forbidden image of Betty crept into his mind.

Mr. Snow stood behind the counter looking at the group like a proud father, thinking how things had changed since he was their age and wishing he could turn back the clock. He walked over to them shook all their hands and wished them well and a Merry Christmas and happy and prosperous New Year. They scattered to begin making a dent into their shopping lists. Downtown Smoky Mountain really looked like a small town to Reggie. He realized he could walk the length of Main Street in ten minutes and there was only a choice of five department stores. But viewing the decorations in store windows, shoppers overloaded with packages and watching Santa in his over stuffed chair in the department stores handing out candy to children brought back memories of Christmas before he discovered there was no Santa Claus. In the distance he heard the sound of the Salvation Army's bells ringing. He suddenly felt free of his troubles and charged off to do his shopping.

When he arrived back home, Mrs. Morton greeted him with a request to go find all the Christmas decorations. That kept his Christmas spirit going. After dinner everyone dug into the large brown box and pulled out the red collapsing bells, the artificial garland, strings of colored light bulbs and a statue of Mary, Joseph and the baby Jesus. The garland and lights were wrapped around the door, the bells hung in the windows, and the manger was arranged on the coffee table. When everything was in place, Mrs.

Morton announced, "Now the Christmas season has officially started at the Morton's house."

When Reggie returned to his room that night, the feeling of loneliness returned. He thought maybe it was because Mona was not there or that he longed for Chicago. He tried to picture what Christmas was like at the Sanders' home. He imagined a tall, live Christmas tree full of colorful light bulbs in the living room with lots of beautifully wrapped presents under it and joyous Christmas music trumpeting through the apartment. His mind shifted to Mona and he wondered what she was doing down in Alabama. He pictured her trying to comfort an ailing grandmother in a rocking chair with a handmade quilt covering her body from shoulders to feet while Dr. and Mrs. Townsend rushed around the house decorating and trying everything possible to capture the spirit of Christmas.

Christmas morning arrived with the smell of fried cured ham with red gravy, rice, homemade sage pork sausages, scrambled eggs and baked Ho Cakes. Reggie was the first to arrive at the table with a clean face and wearing his pajamas. Doug followed still wiping soap from his face and Mr. Morton brought up the rear covered in his housecoat. After breakfast they gathered in the front room where presents had been stacked around the coffee table during the night. Reggie was really surprised. His presents were two pairs of Levi jeans and two plaid shirts.

"Thank you, thank you," he said with glaring eyes and a big smile. He gave his mother a scarf that resembled one he had seen in Chicago, and gave his father a wallet. Doug received a shaving kit with some Mennen aftershave lotion and he gave his parents a set of dishes. Mr. Morton brought out a bottle of his homemade wine and shared it with his sons for the first time. They pretended it was a great surprise; however, both had dipped into it several times in the past and were unimpressed by the taste, but satisfied with the conquest. Christmas dinner included turkey stuffed with oyster dressing, macaroni and cheese, candied yams, collard greens, baked ham, potato salad, and corn bread. After grace was said, all you could hear around the table were the occasional grunts and the, "There ain't no cooking like yours, Mom; you outdid yourself this time."

After dinner Mrs. Morton reminded them about the coconut cake, chocolate cake, jelly cake and sweet potato pie. Nobody responded. They were already losing the battle to stay awake. Mrs. Morton was savoring every moments of this celebration with both of her sons at home.

Doug headed back to base the day after Christmas, while Reggie met his friends again and studied for his final exams. The day after New Years, Reggie was on his way back to school, glad he would not have to tell any more of those half-truths about life at Davis. But he dreaded returning to the stares from students, prejudiced professors and the feeling of isolation. He also wasn't looking forward to Robert finding out about his closer relationship with Harry or the problem of trying to escape the dangers of Betty. But above all, the fear of final exams churned in him.

22

Reggie arrived back on campus around twilight. Students were greeting each other with gloomy faces realizing that they had left their books to collect dust over the Christmas holidays. Now there was nothing between them and those intimidating final exams that were fast approaching. Reggie entered his room and laid down all his bags, including the box filled with turkey, light bread, chocolate cake and sweet potato pie his mother had prepared, but he had not touched. He felt some comfort back in his room. At least he was safe from his mother's complaints about Mr. Sanders and Dr. Hunt and he could share memories of Chicago with Harry. He was determined to do well on his final exams and face Robert and Betty like a man, if necessary. The feeling of hunger surfaced and he dove into that box of food he had been carrying all day.The weeks in January leading up to final exams found Reggie reclaiming his favorite spot in the library. He had heard the first semester exams were tougher than the ones in the spring, which increased his anxiety about maintaining the grade point average necessary to keep his scholarship. Drs. Schulman and Woodcliff had shown no significant change in their attitudes, but he hoped they would muster up some sense of fairness since these grades would be for the record. He felt more secure about his other classes, but he wanted to score high in them to counter any possible low grades from the other two.

The first exams took place on a cold, rainy Monday, the kind of day that suppresses optimism and chokes any positive thinking. The exams for that day were none other than English Composition and Sociology, which made Reggie think the devil had decided to give him undivided attention. He sought comfort through one his mother's favorite expression when facing an unexpected challenge, "Get thee behind me Satan," he said through his clinched teeth and tightened jaws. He then took a deep breath, dressed and left for Richter Hall.

English Composition was the first exam. After Reggie read the questions, he realized that all required essay answers. He felt as he did at midterms; he knew the answers so he wrote until the period was over.

He felt good and declared he should at the least get a strong "C" and hopefully better. There were two hours before the Sociology test. Reggie raced back to his room for a breather and a final review of his notes. The Sociology test was half-essay and half-multiple choice. Reggie thought he aced the multiple choice part, but he prayed his essay answers were so thorough they left no room for Dr. Woodcliff to give him a low grade. The next two days he completed the exams for math, psychology and Physical Education. He felt he had done well on all of them. There was only one left and it was the one Reggie wanted to do his best. He did not want to disappoint Dr. Thorn. When he finished the Physical Education exam, he went back to his room, lay across his bed and drifted into a dream. He had failed all his classes and Dr. Thorn was telling him not to take it so hard and that he should try enrolling at Tennessee State University, the all- Negro school. Reggie woke up with his heart racing and sweat pouring down his back. He looked around to make sure he had been dreaming, gathered his books and walked slowly to the library with double determination to ace the test.

Reggie became so involved in studying he did not realize when just about everyone had left the library. He looked up from his notes and noticed it was ten minutes to nine and the library closed at nine. The librarian was approaching to let him know they were preparing to close. He signaled her that he was about to leave. He gathered his belongings and walked out the door.

A January thaw had come out of nowhere and the night was pleasant with a spring like temperature. The campus was practically deserted. Most students were probably in their rooms cramming for one more exam. Reggie decided he needed to stretch before going to bed so he decided to take the long route back to the dorm. As he passed out of the light of the library, he heard someone call, "Reginald, Reginald." He recognized the voice immediately and suddenly his heart began to race. A chill flashed over his body and then he felt the arrival of sweat in his hands and on the back of his neck. Fear and arousal took hold of him at the same time, each trying to edge out the other. What do I do to handle this like a man? He wondered. "Maybe I should just keep walking and pretend I didn't hear the call." But the sound of her foot steps kept getting closer.

"What are you doing out this late?" Betty asked. Reggie was hoping the war going on inside him would not be revealed in his voice.

"I was just taking a long walk back to the dorm to relax before going to bed. I have one more exam tomorrow and then I am finished. What about you?"

"I was also studying for my last two exams which are tomorrow. May I walk with you?" she asked.

"Of course," Reggie answered, but he really wanted to say, "No! Get thee behind me, Satan!"

"It's such a beautiful night with this full moon why don't we walk down to the garden? It could be very relaxing," Betty suggested. That was the last place Reggie wanted to walk with this white girl at this time of night. He saw trouble flashing like a neon sign in that suggestion. He asked himself, how would a man handle this? God knows what could happen if someone sees us. He was not about to share those thoughts with Betty and destroy his image of someone in control of himself and he was too nervous to think of a dignified escape strategy. It seemed his mouth opened automatically and "okay" rolled off his tongue. And at that moment arousal claimed a victory over fear and he began to fantasize about the possibilities of being alone with Betty in the garden. He tried to fight the thoughts, but they kept slipping in.

"How was your Christmas break?" Betty asked.

"I went home. It was okay," Reggie was feeling too excited to keep up the conversation so they walked in silence for a while.

When they reached the garden, Betty led the way to a bench and sat down. Reggie stood over her trying to maintain some control over the passion he felt. Betty insisted he sit down. He sat about two feet from her. She moved in close, rested her hand on his thigh and Reggie felt like a bolt of electricity had charged through his body. Betty laid her head on his shoulder, kissed him on the neck and whispered in his ear, "Take me Reginald, take me." Any fragment of fear that might have lingered in him threw up a white flag and surrendered to arousal. Reggie pulled her into his arms in a tight embrace and began to kiss her soft lips savagely as she prowled his body to make them one, both holding on passionately until the stars in the sky seemed to explode.

They agreed to leave the garden separately, but Betty made Reggie promise to meet her there Saturday night at ten when there would be no students around. Reggie said, "yes". He would have agreed to anything to escape the situation.

Back in his room, Reggie grew tense thinking of possible consequences. What if someone actually saw them and reported it to the dean? What if Betty became pregnant? What did this mean for his relationship with Mona? How would he handle future contacts with Betty? Would he give in to her again? Should he keep the Saturday night date he had agreed to? Could he sleep tonight and be alert enough to ace Dr. Thorn's test tomorrow? He beat his fist into his hand and turned his head from side to side over and over again saying, "You fool! You fool!"

He didn't remember being sleepy enough to fall asleep, but the clock on his desk indicated it was seven-thirty. His body felt tired and stiff. The test was not until nine-thirty so he decided to dress and go to the student union for some black coffee to get a boost of energy so he could review his notes. It worked. The stiffness eased and he began to feel alert.

Dr. Thorn greeted him as he entered the room. She asked how he was doing with his final exams. He told her he felt things were going well, but he wouldn't really know until the grades were out. Dr. Thorn wished him the best.

When Reggie handed her his blue book on the way out of the exam room, Dr. Thorn said, "You must come see me before you sign up for your spring classes. I might be able to help guide your choices." Reggie assured her that he would. He didn't know what she meant by helping his choices, but he would be happy to listen to whatever she had to say. He felt good about the test; but just to give himself a little more assurance, he prayed, "Oh Lord, please let me ace this one."

When Reggie walked out of Richter Hall, he greeted the return of winter. There was a grey, overcast sky and cold winds that brushed across his face. He had anticipated being elated when the last exam was over. However, the dark day and the onset of fatigue robbed him of those feelings. Instead, his mood was as grey as the day. He wanted to escape to some deserted island away from people with high expectations of him. It felt good closing the door behind him after entering his room. He remembered the album Mrs. Sanders had given him. He put it on, fell onto his bed, and stared at the ceiling as the soothing music filled the room. He fell asleep somewhere around noon, woke up five hours later, went to dinner, returned to his room and tried to write Mona, but he didn't know what to say. After an hour he gave up the effort. He was agitated that he promised to meet Betty at ten Saturday night, which was two days away. He remembered stories about white women who couldn't have their way with a black man and would make up some tall tale about a rape or an attempted rape which was enough to cost the man his life. The thought of Betty doing something like that caused the muscles in his stomach to tighten. He desperately wanted to keep it from happening, but at the moment he didn't know how.

23

THE FRIDAY AFTER EXAMS WAS A TROUBLING DAY. REGGIE WAS WAITING FOR the knock on the door summoning him to the dean's office where he would be confronted with the serious crime he had committed with Betty. He had no defense and was therefore certain he would be sent packing. Whenever he left his room and came in contact with students, he thought they all knew his secret and were waiting to wave him good bye, but Friday passed without the knock. There were also no postcards in his mail box announcing his grade from any of his classes. He had followed the tradition of leaving each professor a self ressed postcard to have his grade mailed since it took a long time to receive them from administration.

Reggie's nights had been restless since his encounter with Betty. His muscles felt sore and no matter how he lay down or sat, he still felt tired. When he opened his sore eyes on Saturday morning hoping for some relief, he suddenly realized it was the day he had to come up with a way of dealing with Betty. As he tossed in the bed, he repeated the prayer, "Please God help me out of this situation and give my head power over my crotch so I will never do this again." He swore he would dedicate himself to his studies and his life with Mona, if the good Lord would deliver him from the tragedy.

He tumbled out of bed, walked over to the window and noticed very little activity. There was no game scheduled that day. The few students he saw were clinging to their coats protecting themselves from the cold winds. The sky was cloudy and there was mist on his window indicating it was not only cold, but also damp. He was in no mood to go outside looking for a distraction from his worries. At noon he went down to check his mailbox. There was a letter from Mona. As he picked up the letter, there were two postcards underneath. His heart began to race.

The first one was from Dr. Schulman's class and it was a "D". He gasped to catch his breath. The second one was Dr. Woodcliff's class and it also was a "D" as if the two had conspired together to defeat him.

Reggie was now angry. He felt certain he had done well enough on those tests to merit at least a "C". He wanted to hurt someone. He dared any white person to cross him. He couldn't wait until Monday to confront those two white crackers. He returned to his room and buried his face into a pillow and repeatedly shouted, "You no good peckerwood crackers, you prejudiced bastards."

When he finally pulled himself together he looked out of the window and it was snowing, an unusual occurrence for Danville. He had not seen snow for years and watching it provided a needed distraction. As the day went on, the snow intensified and suddenly Reggie could see one answer to his prayers. There was no way he could be expected to be in the garden at ten o'clock in this weather. He also realized this was the third day since the encounter with Betty and he had not been called to the dean's office. Maybe that crisis was passing. But he was not about to let those two prejudiced professors off the hook.

After greeting the beautiful fallen snow with snowball fights and building snow men, Sunday found the campus practically deserted. Students were huddled in their rooms away from the howling winds that had followed the snow storm. Reggie looked out over the snow-covered campus; the tree branches yielding to the mounds of snow covering them and glistening icicles hanging from roofs. It looked like a scene on a page in one of those fairy tale books where there was always a happy ending. He remembered the letter from Mona. He picked it up from his desk and walked back to the window as if the tranquil scene would ease his guilt.

The letter told him that New York was beautiful at Christmas and she really enjoyed going down to Rockefeller Center and seeing the tree and the decorations in the stores and store windows, especially Macy's. But Birmingham was depressing. All she did was long to be in Smoky Mountain with him. She couldn't wait for the spring vacation so they could be together. Reggie put down the letter, bit his bottom lip, shook his head from side to side and closed his eyes in shame. He was in no mood to answer it.

Monday finally arrived and Reggie's anger resurfaced. He arrived in Richter Hall at nine-thirty promptly and marched towards Dr. Schulman's office. Dr. Schulman was looking over some papers when Reggie knocked on the door. He said, "Come in." However, when he saw it was Reggie, the look on his face seemed to say, "I won and you lost." As polite as he could manage, Reggie said, "Good morning, sir, I am here about my grade in your class. I had never received a 'D' on any of the work I turned in and I was certain I did well on the final exam. So sir, could you explain how I ended up with a 'D'?"

"Well, Mr. Morton, you obviously overestimated your performance on the final exam which makes up a large part of your final grade."

"Sir, what did I make on the exam?" Reggie asked.

"You did 'D' work on the exam."

"May I see the exam?" Reggie asked.

"We don't pass out final exams," Dr. Schulman responded.

"I am right here, sir, you can hand it to me."

Dr. Schulman rolled his eyes and said, "I am a busy man, Mr. Morton, would you excuse me?" He returned to reading the papers on his desk and left Reggie standing there with anger and hurt in his eyes. Reggie walked outside in the cold for a moment to collect his thoughts and take some deep breaths before confronting Dr.Woodcliff.

He marched to Dr Woodcliff office so angry his body was shaking. When he entered the reception area, Dr .Woodcliff was standing there with a cup of coffee in one hand and a newspaper in the other. He looked up and saw Reggie and his face began to turn red.

"Can I help you?" he said. He could see the anger in Reggie's eyes. He bristled.

"I came to talk to you about my final exam and the 'D' you gave me," Reggie said as he trembled.

Dr. Woodcliff snapped, "I didn't give you a 'D' Mr. Morton; you earned a 'D'."

Reggie asked, "May I see my final exam?"

"I am sorry. You will have to take my word for it. Good day, Mr. Morton," Dr. Woodcliff said as he turned and walked into his office.

Reggie felt like charging into him. He stood in place for a moment then walked out. He started to go and complain to the dean, but quickly squashed that idea; the dean may be waiting to discuss the encounter with Betty, so he walked out of Richter Hall into the howling winds that almost took his breath away, but did not cool him down. He needed a target to strike and he thought an arrogant white person would be ideal. If he could get in one good punch, he might feel better. He was walking with his head down kicking anything that got in his path when he heard, "Mr. Morton." Reggie cupped his fist.

When he looked up Dr. Thorn was closing the door to her car and looking in his direction. Reggie immediately tried to reverse the muscles in his face to hide his anger. Dr. Thorn sensed his mood and figured she knew why; however, she pretended not to notice.

"How are you doing today? Have you completed your exams?" She asked him. Reggie told her they were all done. "Do you know how you did?"

"I did okay," Reggie said without hesitation.

"Well, you received an 'A' in my class," Dr. Thorn said smiling. Reggie's face burst from a frown to a full face smile and he said, "Thank you! Thank you! Thank you!"

"Don't forget my offer," Dr. Thorn said. "I will be glad to advise you on your classes for next semester. Come by my office and set up an appointment if you are interested." Reggie assured her he appreciated anything she could do for him and that he would definitely set up an appointment.

Reggie headed back to the dorm. He stopped by the mailbox before going up to his room and his other grades had arrived. He received a "B" in Psychology, a "C" in Math and an "A" in Physical Education. He wanted to run back out of the dorm and across the campus waving his grades in the air. He bounced to his room and decided to write the overdue letters to Mona and his parents.

He told Mona how much he missed her at Christmas and that his friends asked for her and how much he too looked forward to Easter when they would see each other again. He told her his grades were not everything he wanted, but he was doing okay. He told his mother he had made it through the first semester which they say is the hardest and he was still intact with decent grades and he looked forward to improving next semester. He turned on the LP Mrs. Sanders had given him and enjoyed an excerpt from Beethoven's Fifth Symphony.

The next morning Reggie realized he had slept in the same spot all night. He felt rested, energetic, optimistic and hungry. He dashed off to breakfast and had pancakes, bacon and eggs. When he returned to his room, he found an envelope shoved under the door. The return address showed it was from Dean Jager. Reggie's hands began to shake. He felt those pancakes he just digested had arrived at a stop sign. He wondered if the good Lord had run out of windows to open for him since he was certain another door was about to be slammed shut. He opened the envelope and it merely said Dean Jager wanted to see him at one-thirty today. Surely Betty didn't expect him to come out in that snow, He wondered. Maybe someone saw them and hadn't had a chance to report it until finals were over. It really didn't matter. The curtains were about to fall and he had no idea what he could say or do to defend himself. He wondered what he would tell his parents after they had read his latest letter. How would he explain to Mona or his friends who were led to believe he was doing well? He dreaded even more what the Sanders and Hunts would think of him. He saw his dream of succeeding in Chicago flying out the window and him returning to Smoky Mountain and taking a job alongside his father. He paced the floor, tossed on his bed and beat his fist into his hand until it was time to see Dean Jager.

When Reggie walked into the dean's office, he was greeted by a stone-faced, no nonsense secretary. She looked like she was in her fifties, with salt and pepper hair rolled in a ball on top of her head.

"You are Reginald Morton aren't you?" She said in a very abrupt manner. The fact that she knew his name right off made Reggie more uncomfortable, which he didn't think was possible. "Dean Jager will be with you in a minute. Take a seat."

Reggie did not want to sit because he was sure that if he did, the secretary could see his hands, knees and feet shaking; however, he didn't dare defy her by continuing to stand. He did not have to sit for long.

The secretary instructed Reggie to go in. By this time Reggie's hands were wet and he could feel dampness at the base of his spine. The dean leaned back in a leather chair with his feet on the top of a large mahogany desk that was free of papers except one brown folder labeled, Reginald Morton. He ran his hand over his flat top hair cut and adjusted his brown polka dot bow tie.

"Mr. Morton, you are on an academic scholarship that requires you maintain a 3.0 average to keep it. My records show you completed the fall semester with a two point five average. Your scholarship is over if that can't be raised to three points by the end of the spring semester and you are either out of here or you will have to pay your own way," he said with no sense of concern, empathy or condemnation.

Reggie felt gravity had let go of him, his sins had been wiped away and he was born again. He felt like kissing the dean. He didn't want him to see those feelings and think he was happy so he took a deep breath. "Yes sir, Dean Jager, I understand my situation and I promise I will bring up my average the next semester. Thanks for the warning," he said.

"That will be all Mr. Morton."

Reggie started to reach for his hand to shake it but both of the dean's hands were now clasped behind his head. Reggie was sure his gesture would not be welcomed so he turned on his heels and walked out of the office. When he stepped outside he would have sworn the cold air was warmer and the sun was brighter. He again felt like running across campus, this time shouting like a death row inmate just released from jail.

On his way back to the dorm Reggie bumped into Robert.

"I haven't seen you for a while. What's happening?" Robert asked.

"Just like everybody else, my head has been in the books preparing for finals," Reggie answered.

"Well, how did you make out?" Robert asked.

"I ended up okay. Two of those prejudiced bastards tried to break me and gave me 'D's and wouldn't let me see my final exam to justify their grades, but I scored pretty well in my other classes. I even got an 'A' in American History and Physical Ed. My grade point average is not high enough to hold on to my scholarship and I just came back from Dean Jager's office where I got a warning about losing the scholarship if I didn't bring up my average by the end of next semester."

"Well, it seems like you are riding high, man. They slaughtered me. I only got three 'D's and two 'F's. I am on my way to the dean's office now to hear the sentence. I couldn't do anything right the whole semester. They were out to get me. I was never as bad as they graded me. It's their way of getting rid of me because of Julia. I am not sure I can take it any more. Let me go before I'm late," Robert complained.

"Stop by my room after you leave the dean's office." Reggie suggested.

Reggie felt bad for Robert because he must have had more prejudiced professors than he had and they must have plotted together to make Robert pay for his relationship with Julia. He didn't know how to counsel Robert because if they were determined to get you, they could always claim he could not cut the mustard, especially, if they refused to show you your final exam.

Reggie decided to stop off at the student union to see if Nancy and Sandra were there and find out how they faired with their finals. They were in the corner around the Negro table. He walked over, greeted them and asked if they had completed their exams. Without looking directly at Reggie, Nancy said, "Yes" in a very abrupt manner and returned to looking at the papers in front of her. Reggie asked if they came out okay. Sandra shifted in her seat and said, "Yes," in a very abrupt manner then turned the question on him. Reggie decided they did not want to talk about their grades so he reciprocated by saying, "I did very well."

"So your professor Schulman didn't turn out to be as bad as you thought," Nancy asked with a trace of sarcasm.

"Well, let's say I wouldn't recommend any Negro sign up for his class unless they just want to punish themselves."

"Do you know if Robert made out okay?" Sandra asked, looking directly at Reggie. Reggie's first thought was to answer honestly, but he quickly dismissed that idea and decided he didn't want to spread any more gossip about Robert than was already out there.

"No, I don't know how he did."

Sandra paused for a moment, shook her head in what appeared to be disappointment, and then asked Reggie if he went home for the holidays. Reggie leaned back in his chair and with animation told her about his trip home and the fun he had seeing his family and friends who were home from Howard University and Minnesota. Nancy looked at her watch and said, "We have to go. We'll see you around." Reggie sat for a while, wondering why they continued to treat him as if he were their enemy. They lived in town and knew he was in the dormitory, but they never invited him to anything. He decided they could not get over the way he entered the freshman dance surrounded by a group of white girls. He remembered they also made sarcastic comments about him living in the dorm. Maybe they were jealous, he concluded.

The other Negro students lived in the city and did not spend a lot of time on campus, and since Reggie was the only Negro in his classes there was very little contact with them. Occasionally he would see one or two at the Negro table when he walked through the student union on his way to class. Reggie would always offer a hearty greeting when he came into contact with them. They were always cordial, but never reached out to embrace him and never invited him to any events off campus. This bothered him until his trip to Chicago when he and Harry became close friends.

When Reggie heard the knock on his door he knew it was Robert and he dreaded opening it. He figured Robert's meeting with Dean Jager must have been worse than his. Robert ambled into the room with a sad face and bowed head as if he had been convicted of a crime he didn't commit.

"Well, buddy. I guess this is goodbye," Robert said.

"Did he kick you out?" Reggie asked.

"No, he didn't, but he might as well have. He said, 'your grades indicate you are not prepared for the rigor of Davis and you might want to rethink your choice of schools, and if your grades do not improve by the end of the spring semester, you would be asked to leave; however, you might want to save the money for the spring semester by withdrawing now. The decision is yours'. Low down peckerwood, I wanted to tell him he was full of shit and scared to stink!"

"So have you decided to leave now instead of trying another semester?" Reggie asked.

"I think so; but I didn't tell him. I just walked out. I am going to call my mother and see what she has to say. I really think I would do better with a new start at a new school. I can't win here. They obviously intend to stick it to me until I can't take it anymore."

After Robert left, Reggie decided to go up and check on Harry. Harry opened the door with bloodshot eyes and disheveled hair. "You look like your finals are not over," Reggie said.

"You're right, I have one more tomorrow and when I finish I am going to get drunk," Harry blurted out.

"Well, I am going to let you get back to your studying. We will get together after you finish."

"I will come down and maybe we can find a place that will sell us some beer as soon as I am free again," Harry said.

"Okay, I will be there." Reggie waved him good bye.

Reggie appreciated more than ever that he and Harry had become friends now that Robert was considering leaving and he was beginning to feel relieved that Robert might never find out how close he and Harry had become. But he knew he was going to miss Robert in spite of his discomfort with him. Robert was a Negro who could understand prejudice the way he did. Without someone like Robert around, things could get tougher. He wouldn't know where to begin talking to Harry about prejudice. That would probably be one way of bringing a halt to their friendship. "Well Rev. Bailey, what else do I have to take to make it?" Reggie mumbled to himself.

At seven-thirty the next morning Robert arrived at Reggie's room with his suitcase all packed and a forced smile on his face. "I am out of here today on a nine o'clock bus to Olive Branch. My mother thought I should take off the rest of the semester and apply to Tennessee State University where race will definitely not be an issue. I will enroll as a first semester freshman in the fall. This should clear Davis from my record and I will have a new beginning, another chance to get it right. How about that?" Robert said still forcing a smile. "My mother said Julia had left Olive Branch but she wasn't sure where she had gone so I won't have to face her."

"Well, buddy, I hope things work out for you. I hear they party a lot at Tennessee State and you will have your pick of foxy Negro chicks, but you better make sure you save some time for studying. I am really going to miss you," Reggie said.

"I will keep in touch. Now let me get out of this Hell's den. Don't let them get you," Robert said as he rushed down the hall. Reggie waved him good bye as he began to sniffle. He quickly raised his hand to his eyes to block the tears. He took a deep breath and remembered Dr. Thorn's offer and gathered the course catalog for the spring semester.

Dr. Thorn greeted Reggie with a hearty handshake and a welcoming smile. She questioned him about the subjects he planned to take. After he went over them, she carefully reviewed the class schedules and began to make suggestions about the best time for him to take the class. She never called the name of a professor. It seemed she was avoiding any direct criticism of any of them. Reggie took copious notes and followed her direction without deviation when he went to register. She had advised him to go early to registrations because the recommended classes might fill up quickly. He did and got them all. He walked out of the gym wondering if any recipient of John Bears Tipton's million dollar gift could feel better than he did at that moment.

He was certain Dr. Thorn had led him away from professors like Dr. Schulman and Dr. Woodcliff. He went back to Dr. Thorn and informed her of his success and thanked her. He tried to hide the height of his enthusiasm because it might betray what he considered an unspoken secret between them. Included in Reggie's schedule, of course, was another of Dr. Thorn's classes. When she noticed it, she tried to suppress a smile. She only said, "I look forward to seeing you in class."

Reggie remained the only Negro in his classes; however, students and teachers were more indifferent to him. But there were still some stares whenever he spoke in class. From time to time he could hear "*nigger*" being whispered. Some students would smile and speak to Reggie, but would not invite him to participate in any social activities and absolutely no white student would approach the Negro table in the student union. Except for Dr. Thorn's history classes, it was still hard for him to get an "A" in a course even though he felt he deserved it.

24

Reggie's enthusiasm for his newly found comfort with life at Davis had distracted him from the fact that he had not heard from Mona since the end of the semester. It had been over three weeks and that was unusual, even though the frequency of her letters had tapered off. He decided to write and ask what was going on in New York. Two more weeks passed and she had not answered. Reggie was now worried something unpleasant had happened. He wondered if it had anything to do with school or with her family. He decided to send off another letter informing her he was worried and needed to hear something. Another week passed before the letter from Mona arrived. It began "Dear Reggie" instead of the usual "My dear Reggie." The greeting shot through him, jangling his nerves. He was reluctant to read on. She apologized for taking so long to answer his letters but said preparing for final exams had taken up all her free time. She was depressed after the exams because she did not do as well as she had expected. She went on to say she had had a bad cold that confined her to bed for a few days. And then she dropped the bomb.

She told him she had been seeing someone for a while and it had become serious and she no longer wanted to mislead him. She explained that they were friends that found themselves in love one day. She went on to say she planned to visit his parents in Los Angeles during spring break. She ended by asking his forgiveness, telling him he was her first love which would be a memory she would always cherish, and how she looked forward to reading about him breaking barriers in the corporate world and being married to a devastatingly beautiful woman.

Reggie sat in a daze. His vision became blurred. The room suddenly seemed cold and he began to tremble. He felt sad, abandoned, betrayed, and lonely. He felt angry, inadequate and confused. He wanted to hold Mona in his arms and tell her how much he loved her. He wanted to slap her face and tell her to come to her senses and remind her of the commitment they made to each other. Tears welled in his eyes as he paced the floor with the letter in his hand. He thought of running to Betty and asking her to love him. He wanted to telephone Mona and ask her to come back to him. Writing a letter and waiting for an answer was more than he could handle.

As the tears were finally released, Reggie began to think Mona's decision was too abrupt. He wondered how long this relationship had been going on to have developed to love and how could she have been so convincing in her letters that she was still in love with him? How could she play with his heart that way? What kind of person was she? Who was this guy that had stolen her heart? Was he from a family like Mona's? Did her parents put her up to it? Reggie felt something was missing in Mona's account and he needed more details. He sat down and wrote a letter expressing his love, anger, confusion and asking how this could happen?

After completing the letter, he walked outside to the mail box, opened the lid, and held it for a while wondering if the effort was worth it. After all, he never really felt secure he could hold on to her. He started to walk towards the garden, but the winds were too cold and his last memory of the garden would only make his present situation worse. He felt restless and wanted to talk to another person; however, his options were limited. Robert would have understood if he was here, but he was gone and there was only Harry. He felt desperate. Maybe I need to take a chance, he thought. He dropped the letter in the box and walked up to Harry's room and knocked on the door.

When Harry answered he noticed the distressed look on Reggie's face and asked him what was wrong.

Reggie asked him if he felt like going for a walk. Harry immediately agreed, but he felt anxious. This was a new role for him. Nobody had ever asked him to listen to their troubles; he was used to the reverse. He was flattered, but not exactly sure what to do or say, so he kept quiet. Reggie poured out his feelings about Mona and how he did not want to lose her. When he got it all out, there was a pause. Harry thought he had found some wisdom and said, "There are many fish in the sea. Can you imagine going through life and catching only one?"

Reggie looked at him almost in surprise, smiled and said, "No."

Mona never did answer Reggie's letter. Even though he always thought there was the possibility the relationship would end that way, it didn't lessen the pain he still felt. He decided love was too painful for him and he didn't want to experience it again.

His mother's letter arrived on schedule. She told him how happy she was about the outcome of his final exams and grades and how proud everyone back home was about his success at Davis. She said his father sends his love and they had received a letter from Doug who had gone overseas but still seemed to be enjoying the Army.

"Son," she continued, "I have been wondering if you heard from Mona. Rumors are she got herself pregnant by a white man named Michael Conan, a senior at Columbia University. What a shame, after her parents spent all that money sending her to New York to go to a rich school. I understand Mr. Conan is from Los Angeles, California, and they are getting married. Mona is going to live with his parents until he graduates this spring. If the rumors are true, and I have no reason to doubt them, I figured you would be upset. I was hoping she was woman enough to tell you. Now, don't you go worrying yourself, there are plenty of nice girls out there that would love having a man like you."

This was a scenario Reggie had not considered. He didn't want to believe the rumors. He wanted to believe they were being spread by people who disliked the Townsends. He wanted to call Mona and ask her to deny it. He wondered how such rumors could ever get started. What could have caused people to say things like that? Then he remembered how he thought something was missing in Mona's story. He now felt sad because he believed she really did love him, but could not face him with what she had done. He knew his love for her was as strong as ever in spite of it all. Maybe if I confessed my deeds she would know I understand and come back to me, he thought. But somehow, he couldn't escape the feeling that, as much as he wanted to hold on, it was too late and he had to let go.

Reggie didn't want to face Smoky Mountain where he knew that people would be looking at him with pity. He didn't feel up to hearing the "I can't believe this" comments from his friends, so he decided to skip spring break. He told his mother he had too much work to do. He would not tell Harry his plans because he was certain Harry would insist on him going to Chicago and he was not ready to be positive around the Sanders and Hunt families. He spent the time trying to work on term papers and doing some studying, but it was hard to concentrate. By the middle of the week, he couldn't figure out which was worse, facing people who might share his grief or wallowing in it alone. He couldn't believe the day would come when he would welcome the resumption of classes.

25

As soon as Harry returned to campus, he went straight to Reggie's room, full of excitement. "Reggie, guess what? Dr. Hunt said he has a job for you this summer if you want it and my parents asked me to encourage you to take it because it would give you a head start on a job after graduation. What do you say? Think, a whole summer in Chicago, you could really see what its like. Say you will go." Reggie thought this must be the window God opened after Mona closed the vault. He wanted to immediately accept the offer. It would keep him out of Smoky Mountain until the talk about Mona faded, and he had been dreaming of returning to Chicago. He wondered how his parents would feel since he did not go home for spring break, especially considering how his mother felt about the Sanders and Hunts.

"I think it's a great idea. Let me talk to my parents and I will let you know," Reggie said.

When Reggie presented the idea to Mrs. Morton, she was distressed. She didn't want Reggie to ever see those people in Chicago again and she resented that he needed the money they couldn't give him. She also realized he could not get any job worthwhile in Smoky Mountain for the summer so she begrudgingly agreed. "Promise me you will come home before you return to school," she requested. Reggie readily agreed and dashed to Harry's room to give him the good news.

The rest of the semester went fast and before he realized the time, finals were facing him again. Reggie felt confident this time. Dr. Thorn's guidance had been a life saver. The semester had gone by without any memorable indications that he had grossly unfair professors. Two days before he was scheduled to leave for Chicago those all-telling postcards arrived. Reggie immediately computed his grade point average and understood that he had made it. The scholarship had been saved. He danced around the room throwing the cards in the air. He was ready to return to Chicago and tell the Sanders and Hunts about his grades, which would assure them that their opinions of him were correct.

There was a white envelope with the cards. He picked it up off the floor. It did not have a stamp and the writing was not familiar. He ripped it open. There was a very short message, "I will be going home for the summer tomorrow, please meet me in the stadium on the south side in section five, first row, tonight at nine o'clock. The weather is no excuse this time. Betty."

The description of the time and place to meet caused Reggie to become aroused. He held the note in his hand and began to pace the floor. He knew he had promised God he would never put himself in that situation again and he did not want to feel his wrath. But, he thought, no one saw them the last time and obviously Betty had not betrayed him. Maybe he could trust her or maybe she was sent by God. He tried to tell himself over and over he was being stupid and reckless, but his nature would not retract.

They met and made love on the grassy surface behind the stadium, watched only by the stars, the moon, and the cool spring breeze that flowed constantly over their bodies.

"I look forward to seeing you in the fall," Betty said while walking away.

Reggie watched her hair flowing around her shoulder and her hips swaying as she disappeared out of sight. He realized those secret out-of-the-sight-of-people encounters with Betty could be dangerous, but passion had conquered fear each time. Maybe it could happen more often; maybe he was falling in love with Betty, he thought. He was sure, however, his feelings were not as strong as those he felt for Mona, but Mona was gone.

26

THE SANDERS WELCOMED REGGIE WITH A SPECIAL MEAL PUT TOGETHER BY Consuelo. She had rice with beans, which Reggie thought was strange. His rice had always stood alone, and so had his beans. The succulent Barbecue ribs grabbed his attention. It seemed Consuelo had picked them up at a rib shack on Chicago's South side. There was smothered cabbage that was not limp enough for Reggie and he kept forking through them, looking for the okra that was noticeably absent. And for dessert, they hit the mark: cheesecake. Everybody ate as if it were one of their regular meals, except Mr. Sanders only took one rib. Reggie ate heartily and praised the meal. "Thank you," Mrs. Sanders said with a proud smile.

The next morning Harry took Reggie on the train to Dr. Hunt's office. Dr. Hunt greeted Reggie as if he were a new patient with a serious disease he knew he could cure. He explained to Reggie that he had been accepted into a management training program at Rodman Advertising. The program would expose him to various aspects of management, which would prepare him for management positions in advertising or some other industries. He could continue the program over the next two summers if he was interested. Reggie assured him that he would like nothing better.

"Rodman is just a few blocks from here so we can walk and I can show you how to get there," Dr. Hunt said. He pointed out the train station where he would get off and the directions to the tall building they were approaching. When they got off the elevator on the fourteenth floor and began walking down the hall, Reggie saw that Rodman was not exactly what he thought a business would be like. The offices were not the same. One had a rocking chair, another had a barber's chair, and another had a complete Hi-fi system with jazz music playing. Some of the men wore three piece suits while others wore open collar sport shirts. Reggie's immediate supervisor was a white woman in her thirties. She was in one of those offices Reggie expected: straight back chair, desk, sofa, coffee table and a bookcase. There were papers spread all over the place. Next to her desk was an extra pair of shoes. She seemed a bit nervous or maybe just disorganized. She stood up as Dr. Hunt and Reggie entered the office.

"Good morning, Sara, this is Reginald Morton, the young man I spoke to you about. Reggie, this is Sara Bentley. She will be your supervisor this summer."

"You may call me Sara. May I call you Reggie?" She asked while reaching to shake his hand and pat him on the shoulder.

"Yes, Ma'am," Reggie answered.

"I'm going to leave you two to your work," Dr. Hunt said and excused himself.

"I'll take good care of him." Sara said.

"I understand you are from Smoky Mountain, Tennessee, and a sophomore at Davis University. It must be really exciting for you to be working in Chicago. I think you are really going to like it here. This is an exciting business. We are going to expose you to as much as we can this summer. Are you ready?"

"Yes Ma'am."

"Don't forget, call me Sara."

"Yes Ma'am. Oh, I mean Sara. I'm really grateful for this opportunity and I promise you I will work hard and try to learn everything you teach me."

"I am sure you will. Come with me I'll show you around." Everybody gave him a hearty hello, a smile and handshake when Sara introduced him. They came to a large room with what looked like four drawing tables and high stools. "This is our Bullpen," Sara said. Reggie thought that was a strange name for an office. He wanted to laugh, thinking maybe these four men were considered studs. He was hoping this was not the place she was going to dump him. One of the men was a Negro and Sara walked straight up to him and said, "Walter I want you to meet Reggie Morton. He will be with us this summer in our intern program."

Walter grabbed Reggie's hand with both of his and said, "Welcome aboard, I'm Walter Washington. After you get all settled, let's get together for lunch."

"I look forward to it." Reggie said.

After the tour, Sara showed Reggie his office which was two doors down the hall from hers. It had two chairs, a desk, a cabinet and a telephone. "A private office with my own telephone. Wow!" he silently gloated. Sara explained he would be getting assignments from her each day and they would meet periodically to go over the things he was working on. She told him that her door was always open and he could come in any time and ask questions. She then gave him a notebook about Rodman and instructed him to get settled and go over the material.

As soon as Sara walked out and closed the door, Reggie sat down at his desk. "I wish I could take a picture of this and send it to Mom, Dad and the gang," he thought. "I bet they would get a kick out of it." He stood up, walked around the small office and looked out the window into the busy city with bustling crowds. Each person seemed to be heading to some destination to do their part to make the city, the country, or the world work for all of us. "It's time to start doing my part," he declared and opened the book Sara had given him.

There were advertisements for Bright White Detergent, the kind his mother used, floating soap, and Good Morning Cereal, all products that were familiar to the folks in Smoky Mountain. *Well, here I am. What do you know, Reggie Morton, the little poor Negro from Smoky Mountain, Tennessee working in Chicago in a company with smart people responsible for selling products the whole country knows about. Is this what you call making it, Rev. Bailey? Maybe I should send the Townsends a postcard.* He continued to thumb through the book wondering what it would be like working with such smart people, what his assignments would be and whether he could handle them. He decided that he could work night and day if necessary to measure up.

"Hey man, have you worked up a sweat yet?" Walter asked standing in the doorway. "How about some lunch before you pass out?"

"No, the sweat hasn't shown up, but I have worked up an appetite," Reggie said.

"Okay, follow me. I know a nice place with good cheap food."

"Let me tell Sara," Reggie said.

"No need, she went to a meeting. I told her I would take you to lunch. You are all set."

The restaurant, MaMa Mexico, was about five blocks from the office, perched between an Irish bar with pictures of the green hills of Ireland hanging in the windows and the sound of rowdy voices rushing out the doors each time they opened. On the other side was a small café with a line of stools at the counter and a Negro woman in a yellow uniform taking orders. Reggie thought he got a whiff of chitlins when the door opened and it perked his appetite. He thought he noticed Walter turn up his nose. The menu in the window of MaMa Mexico showed the restaurant served Mexican food with some continental dishes, but when Reggie walked in the sharp smells of spicy food rising from the plates on each table filled the air. In the background the sound of guitars releasing romantic melodies floated through the restaurant, muffling the lunch time chatter. The crowd consisted of a mixture of races, but most of them were white. The waitresses, dressed in colorful uniforms with puffy sleeves, rushed from the kitchen to the tables with serious looks, occasionally interrupted by a forced half smile. A man with a heavy accent directed Reggie and Walter to a table covered with a red table cloth and plaid napkins. "Okay, Senores?" He asked and handed them a menu.

"Okay," Walter said.

"Have you had Mexican food before?" Walter asked.

"Well, I have had some hot tamales," Reggie said, a little embarrassed.

"I bet the ones here will top the ones you had. Also make sure whatever you order includes the refried beans. You won't be sorry," Walter advised.

"People in Chicago really do funny things with beans. The other night I had rice and beans and now you are telling me Mexicans fry them. How about me trying the refried beans another day and ordering a hamburger and French fries today?"

"Okay, but you've got to open up. You're in the big city now with all kinds of options."

Walter looked to be in his early twenties. He was tall, good looking with a deep voice. He was an artist, as Reggie found out, and had worked at Rodman for two years. He immediately started telling Reggie that Rodman was a tough place to work and he needed to keep his eyes opened. He explained that what you see is not always what is meant. A smile is sometimes just a cover for some hidden sinister feeling. "I once came up with ideas for an advertising campaign and discussed it with some of the guys in my area who praised me for thinking of it. The next thing I knew my boss was praising the idea and thanking one of the other guys for coming up with it. This is the kind of business you are in. I know you must have noticed there are only a few of us there. I believe the only reason I got in was they were in some bind and somebody must have quit or was fired when they needed him the most. I got a call, almost two months after I applied, asking if I could start the next day. Man, I was down there the next morning before they opened the doors. I got in but I would be willing to bet about fifty percent of the people don't want Negroes there and the other fifty percent can't figure out what to do with us or how far to let us go without getting some flack from their clients.

"Okay, now that I have scared you on your first day, let me give you a security blanket to wrap around you. Well maybe not a whole blanket. Let's say a pillow case to cover your head. You can make good money in this business if they let you, and Negroes love to know you are breaking the racial barrier and paving the way for others in this small, elite business. You also get to do things people see all over the country. My best advice is to keep your head on straight, your eyes open, and you will be okay. Don't be afraid to ask questions. Learn everything you can. There will come a time when you will have a chance to show off what you know and they will be shocked and say to themselves, 'that nigger ain't as dumb as he looks.'"

Reggie sat listening intensively. He kept thinking of all those people he met who smiled and shook his hand, which ones meant it and which ones were waiting to do him harm. He remembered he smiled back. Did they think he had some hidden agenda or was he just some green hick from the South who has no idea what he is in for?

"Thanks, man, I will keep my eyes opened and eat up every piece of knowledge I can," Reggie said. But he was thinking Walter's description meant this place must be full of Schulmans and Woodcliffs. They just know how to smile.

"Hey, man, where are you staying? Maybe we can hang out sometimes. I can introduce you to some of these Mexican senoritas."

Reggie explained his living situation.

"Man! It looks like you've got it made. The people at Rodman probably won't mess with you. You know you could bring along your buddy Harry when we go out," Walter said.

"Yes, I'll think about it," Reggie answered.

Throughout the summer Reggie got so many smiles from people who were more than willing to help with any request or question; he decided most were probably real. He certainly had not seen any recrimination, and it was so different from Drs. Schulman and Woodcliff that he wanted to believe they really accepted him.

Sara mostly hauled him to meetings and asked him to take notes and remind her of any follow-up required. He was taken on sets where commercials were being shot. It was the most fascinating thing he had ever seen. He never realized how much everything was staged and how the actors had to keep doing things until the director said it was right. He could not wait for the actual commercials to be aired on television so he could tell people he was there when it was made.

Reggie and Sara developed a good relationship over the summer. He concluded her smile was genuine, but she was often too busy to answer his questions or go over anything with him. The program was unstructured so it was hard for him to tell if he was getting anyplace. He kept notes on everything and reviewed them constantly so he would be ready to flaunt his knowledge when the opportunity came. It seemed he was the only person in the training program that summer so there was no one with whom to compare experiences. Dr. Hunt kept telling him he was getting good reports from Sara. Reggie wondered what she was measuring, but it felt good to hear Dr. Hunt was not disappointed.

"Hey Harry, you remember Walter, the guy I told you about that works with me," Reggie said one night. "Well his girlfriend, Carmen, is having a party Friday night and we are invited. Do you want to go?"

"Yes, I don't have anything planned." But the invitation scared him. His first though was that this could be like going to a country where a peace treaty had been signed, but there was still a lot of hostility against the victor which he represented. He wondered whether someone would get drunk and take out their anti-white feelings on him if there were no other white people there. He could not think of any good reason to get out of going, so he decided he had to swallow his medicine.

It had been a great summer so far, in Harry's opinion. He and Reggie had roamed the city, went to a Cubs game, beached at the Lake, and partied with his friends. He had shown Reggie the ins and outs of riding the El train and Reggie was using it like he grew up with it. Reggie would often meet him at the Walgreens Drug Store where he was working in the Pharmacy Department, getting exposure to his chosen profession. They would then hang out. Now, he felt he was facing the first challenge of the summer.

He hoped Reggie would come to his defense if anything happened at the party so he decided his best strategy was to stick close to him.

At the party, Carmen greeted them with a, "Buenos noches caballeros, bienvenido." Reggie was knocked off balance and tried to muster up a friendly, "Hey," but before he could let it roll out, Harry jumped in with, "*Como estas, senorita.*" He suddenly remembered the Spanish he learned in high school. You could see the anticipation melt away from his face. Carmen's brown eyes sparkled as she reached for his hand and then for Reggie's.

"I'm glad you guys could make it. Come on in and join the party."

"Hey, man, I see you found your way," Walter said, appearing from behind Carmen. Reggie leaped in and introduced Harry, trying to appear composed.

"Food is on the table and drinks are in the kitchen. Come, I will show you," Carmen said as she reached for Harry's hand.

The loud sound of guitars accompanying melodious tenor voices permeated the crowded apartment filled with people of different ages laughing, dancing, and speaking Spanish seemingly in competition with the music." Reggie swayed in place to the rhythm of the music. It didn't matter that he did not understand one word of the lyrics. Carmen dashed off with Harry, leaving Reggie and Walter taking in the scene. Reggie looked across the room and noticed Carmen trying to teach Harry to Rumba. He remembered that night at the Freshmen dance when he was frightened he would have no one to dance with. Harry must be having a good time, he decided. Walter asked Reggie what he thought of the senorita in the tight blue dress with long black hair – the one that kept looking in their direction.

"She looks like flesh I want to hold next to mine," Reggie said.

"That's Carmen's younger sister, Maria. I can introduce you. See the dude with the slick black hair wearing brown pants and the yellow flowered shirt? He likes to think Maria is his property, but she doesn't agree. The way she keeps looking at you I think she might not mind you holding her flesh against yours. Come on I'll introduce you."

"Okay," Reggie said, but he was thinking, "I sure want to hold her, at least one time, but Lord knows I don't want my throat cut." That guy has a lot of muscles and looks mean. I wonder if he is a member of one of the street gangs.

"Maria, I want you to meet my friend, Reggie. He works with me down at Rodman."

"Hello," Maria said, in unaccented English, as she batted her eyelashes and let go a slight smile.

"I'll be right back," Walter said while walking towards Carmen, who had released Harry into the hands of another girl who had him cornered in conversation. The music turned into a ballad conducive to a slow dance. Even though Reggie was apprehensive about making it with Maria, he was not about to miss this opportunity to hold her in his arms so he said, "I'm glad to meet you. This is really a great party. Would you like to dance?"

Maria nodded.

They swayed off to the dance floor under the watchful eye of the guy in the brown pants who stood with his arms folded, teeth clasped and jaws tight. Reggie closed his eyes and held Maria as close as possible. When the music stopped, he opened his eyes and there stood the guy in the brown pants reaching for Maria's hand. She dropped her head without saying anything to Reggie and followed him. Reggie knew what side his bread was buttered on so he put aside all his thoughts of making love to this beautiful woman with olive skin, long black hair, luscious lips and a body that would not quit.

Harry made his way over to where Reggie was standing with his eyes all shiny and said, "This party is really cool." Reggie put his arm around Harry's shoulder and said, "I agree." They both spent the rest of the evening dancing with the different girls that asked them. Every now and then Walter would pull himself away from Carmen and ask Reggie and Harry if they had received a certificate from a Mexican dance school. Reggie would give him the peace sign.

"Good morning you guys," Mr. Sanders said. "Come on in and get your breakfast. I was hoping I would have a chance to see Reggie before he returned home. I have been so busy lately I haven't had a chance to talk to him. You guys must have had a great celebration last night. I turned out my light around two and hadn't heard you come in." A whiff of a smile tried to cross his face. Reggie proudly announced that he had taken Harry to a party. Mr. Sanders asked who gave the party. Reggie quickly blurted out, Carmen Lopez. Mr. Sanders repeated the word, "Lopez," with a very stern look as if to clarify what he had heard. Harry stepped in and said, "I really had a great time." Mr. Sanders again tried to let a smile squeeze from his face and said, "I am glad you guys enjoyed yourselves. Maybe when you return Reggie we will introduce you to some people who will really show you a serious good time. In any event, Dr. Hunt tells me you have made quite an impression at Rodman. We are proud of you and are happy you have decided to continue in the program for the next two summers. That 'B' average you maintained at the end of your first year was a great accomplishment. Keep at it young man. You are going to do well. We wish you all the luck in your second year and, of course, we look forward to seeing you next summer." Mr. Sanders rose from the table to head for the office. "Thank you sir, and I want to thank all of you for your help. I'm beginning to like Chicago as much as you do," Reggie said.

After breakfast, Reggie hugged Mrs. Sanders and thanked her again for all her kindness. Consuela popped out of the kitchen door to say goodbye. Harry then escorted Reggie to the station and told him that he would see him in a few weeks.

27

Reggie retuned to Smoky Mountain with a sack of stories of his life in advertising. After hearing about his office in a tall skyscraper and how commercials were made, the adults in the neighborhood would tell him how proud they were of him and how they looked forward to his finishing college and coming back to Smoky Mountain to help other Negro children follow his path. He loved the compliments but was agitated by the expectation that he would return to Smoky Mountain after graduation.

Mrs. Morton insisted that Reggie go to church with her. She wanted to hear Rev. Bailey announce to the congregation that Reggie was home for a few days before returning to Davis University and asking him to stand and let the congregation welcome him. Reggie dressed in his blue suit, white shirt and pink tie and posed in the mirror from different angles. He tried several facial expressions then walked out of his room to face his public. Mrs. Morton led him into the church a few minutes late and marched him down the aisle to a front row seat.

After reminding the congregation of the upcoming revival and that dinners would be sold Friday night to raise money for the building funds, Rev. Bailey said, "You all know our youth is our hope for the future. Well, Mr. Reggie Morton, who has finished his first year at Davis University and spent the summer working at a big time advertising firm in Chicago, is worshipping with us today. He is a good example of what we want for our young people and what our community needs these days. Thank the Lord he still has a mind to honor God. Sister Morton, we know you are proud and we are proud with you. Mr. Morton, why don't you stand and let us greet you."

Reggie stood up and bowed with a stern look, trying to portray someone who had matured. The congregation said, "Amen" and began to clap. Mrs. Morton sat with her head upright and her back straight, sporting a restrained smile.

A half hour into the service, Reggie began to feel restless. The choir sounded out of tune and just plain loud. Rev. Bailey kept repeating himself, getting louder each time until he got a series of "Amens" or a couple of women shouting down the aisles. Each shouter would be monitored by neatly dressed ushers in starched white dresses ironed to perfection and wearing white gloves. They were poised to rescue any shouter who seemed to be headed for a dangerous fall. Reggie began to shift in his seat and play with his program. Occasionally, Mrs. Morton would cast her eyes in his direction. After the service, members came up to Reggie to congratulate him by shaking his hand and patting him on the back. He thanked each of them and released a strained smile.

Arnold was packing to get back to Washington when the phone rang and Reggie's voice was on the other end. "Hey brother when did you get in town? I'm on my way back to school but we have to get together. Why don't you hook up with Alfred and come by," Arnold said.

"We will see you soon," Reggie answered.

Arnold's racial pride seemed to have moved to a higher level. He only wanted to talk about when the revolution comes and Negroes would take over and how it was time for Negroes to use their economic power to get equal rights. He said Negroes need to start appreciating their rich history that the white man has tried so long to suppress.

Reggie thought Arnold sounded something like his mother when she was attacking Mr. Sanders and Dr. Hunt and it sounded scarier coming from him. Arnold was so wrapped up in his own thing that he never once asked Reggie how he was doing. Reggie was relieved that the subject of Mona never came up, but he was disappointed that Arnold did not seem to be interested in his achievements at Davis. It almost seemed as if he were trying to let Reggie know he was ashamed of him for going to Davis. Whenever

Alfred got a chance to get a word in, he only wanted to talk about buying a Cadillac and luring women.

Reggie didn't want to be alienated from his old friends, but it seemed that things were changing and he was not sure where to lay the blame. He wondered if Arnold and Alfred were holding back the whole truth about their experiences in college as he had, or if he was feeling overly sensitive since he was deliberately holding back. Maybe Howard University was giving Arnold the education Negroes needed to survive and Davis could not do the same for him. But Negroes have fought hard for integration and battles were being won and he was the recipient of one of those battles. How could what I am doing be wrong? Should my black pride rise as high as Arnold's while I am at Davis? He pondered. He began to feel the loss of the camaraderie he used to have with Arnold and Alfred and it left him feeling abandoned.

Mrs. Morton noticed the change in her son. She questioned whether it was the result of growing into manhood or his higher education. But she strongly suspected it represented the growing influence of those misguided folks in Chicago. What she did know for sure was that her influence seemed to be losing ground. She did not know how to stop the ebb, so in frustration, she turned to God and asked Him to guide her and Reggie.

Just as Reggie was preparing to return to school, Beverly arrived in town with a friend. She had spent the summer working in Minnesota. She called and invited Reggie over for dinner. Her call sent a stroke of euphoria through Reggie. He could not wait for the opportunity to talk to her. He wanted to know if things were still as good as she described at Christmas, and he was ready to give her some of the truths about Davis since he had second semester grades to be proud of. He was hoping that she had reached a point where she could understand some of the things he had endured.

When Reggie arrived, he was introduced to Deborah, Beverly's friend, a white girl from Madison, Wisconsin. She was thin, about five feet, six inches, with short brown hair. She was more fashionable than Beverly, but would not be considered chic. She seemed comfortable in an all-Negro environment and freely engaged in conversation with everyone. She couldn't stop talking about how she and Beverly did everything together and how much they had in common. She looked at Beverly with deep admiration. Beverly would sit back and take it all in. You could tell by the expression on her face that she loved every bit of it.

Beverly's parents did not seem as comfortable with Deborah. Her father would fold his arms and cross his legs whenever Deborah showered Beverly with compliments. Her mother would twitch and shake her head. Deborah announced that she and Beverly planned to hitchhike through Europe the next summer. Beverly's mother exploded.

"That doesn't make any sense. It's too dangerous. Where would you stay? Where would you get the money to afford something like that, Beverly? I absolutely forbid it."

"Students do it all the time," Deborah said. "It's neither dangerous nor expensive. They have places where students stay in every country."

"Thank you Deborah, but I'm speaking to my daughter," Mrs. Miller snapped.

"Mother"! Beverly cried out.

"No, No, I am very sorry. I didn't mean any disrespect. I am truly sorry," Deborah pleaded.

"Don't worry about it," Mrs. Miller said. "I just don't think Beverly is as sophisticated as you." She stood up quickly and began to clear the table. Deborah insisted on helping and disappeared into the kitchen behind Mrs. Miller.

Deborah had usurped the evening and now it was time for Reggie to leave. Beverly said she would walk with him part of the way home. They ended up talking for hours about old times and their new lives in integrated schools. The conversation was so refreshing that Reggie only emphasized the positive sides of his life at Davis. Beverly told Reggie that she met Deborah during the spring semester and that they were immediately drawn to each other and had become the closest of friends. But they were still working through stereotypes about each other's race which constantly popped up. She said that she did not want to bring

Deborah home, knowing how her parents would react, but Deborah insisted she wanted to meet them. Deborah's parents had welcomed her in their home and treated her like an honored guest.

Reggie told Beverly that the guy he went home with at Thanksgiving was the closest friend he had on campus. He described how the Sanders and Hunts had taken an interest in him and had gotten him the job he had that summer. He told her he really wanted to live in Chicago when he graduated, thanks to the Sanders, but he was sure his parents wanted him to return to Smoky Mountain. "Can you imagine coming back to Smoky Mountain after you graduate?" Reggie asked.

"No, I can't. I think if I had to return to Smoky Mountain, I would consider myself a failure," Beverly said.

"I know what you mean. You should have been at church with me last Sunday. You would have gotten a kick out of the service. Every time Rev. Bailey said 'Lord' three times, the Amens thundered throughout the church. I couldn't figure out what they were agreeing with. Just as the Amens tapered off you could count on Sister Taylor rising to the floor with her hands in the air shouting, 'Thank you, Thank you, Lord.' If that didn't get her enough attention, the ushers would brace themselves because she would soon be rolling down the aisles as if she were at the Gay Hawk Saturday night when the music got hot. Even if the aisles were full of other shouting sisters, you couldn't miss Sister Taylor. She was the one in the loud red dress that you could see a mile away. Have you ever been some place where she was invited? Well, you should never expect her to show up until everything has been going on for at least an hour. And it is not enough to be late, she walks in speaking so loud you would think she was talking to someone in another neighborhood," Reggie said.

"I can't imagine why anyone would want to make such a spectacle of themselves. It's so *black*," Beverly said.

"Exactly," Reggie agreed. "When will our people ever learn?"

For the first time since that day they discussed the Brown decision in class and his friends teased him about wanting to go to an integrated school, Reggie felt some vindication. He was not out of touch with all of his friends.

PART IV-THE EPIPHANY

28

At the beginning of the semester, Reggie received a letter from the Committee for Centennial Planning. He couldn't imagine what was in the business-sized envelope addressed to Mr. Reginald Morton. Maybe it was something they sent to all students. He slowly tore it open and could not believe what he read. It described some of Davis' proud history, including how it had expanded over the past hundred years and cited some of its distinguished alumni. There was no mention of its struggle with desegregation. The letter ended by inviting Reggie to join the student committee and gave him the date and time of the first meeting. It was signed by the president. The culminating event would take place when he was a senior, so this was a long commitment.

A feeling traveled through Reggie that he thought must be what Christians experience when they say they have been born again. He felt the school's inner circle had finally invited him in. It was the moment he envisioned when Miss Wright gave him the opportunity to announce the Brown decision. He danced around the room, kissing the letter and singing, "Our Day Will Come." Maybe I should send Arnold the letter so he could read it. "Damn him!" Reggie declared.

Reggie was curious as to how he was selected for the Committee, but it was not something he was going to dwell on. However, he strongly suspected it was something that had been promoted by Dr. Thorn. He wanted to shower her with thanks, but was reluctant since he was not sure and he did not want to embarrass her if he was wrong. When her class ended the next day, he stayed after and shared the good news. She nodded and said, "I think that was a good decision and I am sure you will be a great asset."

"I will do my best and thanks for your encouragement."

"You are perfectly welcome, Mr. Morton," Dr. Thorn said emphatically.

Reggie was nervous when he went to the first meeting. One third of the members came over to him, shook his hand and said that they were glad to have him on the committee; one third came into the room and began to talk to other students that they seemed to know without saying anything to him; and another third looked at him and moved to the other side of the room.

During successive meetings, he always found his way to a seat close to someone friendly, but he was mostly ignored during discussion, even by the friendly ones. In those rare instances when his opinion was sought, he looked for something one of the friendly members had said and agreed with it. He was afraid to assert an independent thought and stand out in the group. Occasionally he was invited to join the group for a burger after meetings. One day as they were gathered around a table in the student union far away from the Negro table, one member of the group made the statement, "How could those students doing sit-ins at lunch counters expect to change the law by breaking the law?"

Reggie tensed up. He wondered if he was expected to answer the question. It seemed a reasonable one but he was afraid to speak. Some of the friendly students began to look at each other.

"Remember the Boston Tea Party, when the colonists dumped British tea in the river and started the American Revolution?" one of the students asked. The group went silent and Reggie breathed a sigh of relief.

On another occasion a student talked about how the rising boxing champion, Cassius Clay, was giving new life to the dying sport of prize fighting. Another student jumped in and said he was the worst thing that could happen to boxing. Reggie just listened. He was embarrassed by Cassius Clay. He reminded him of Sister Taylor with his loud voice and boisterous behavior. Reggie did not want the students to associate him with that kind of behavior.

The Civil Rights movement exploded around the country. In addition to the sit-in demonstrations at lunch counters, young Freedom Riders, Negroes and whites, flooded the South, determined to break down segregated accommodations in interstate transportation and to register Negroes to vote. The Black Power Movement was appearing on the horizon and black nationalism was taking a hold in the country. The word Negro was abandoned and "black" became the politically correct term to refer to the descendents of African slaves. "Black is beautiful" became a slogan symbolizing the movement, and kinky hair, once a symbol of shame, became a symbol of pride.

For Reggie, the movement spreading all around him was like a cumulus cloud. He knew it could bring lightning and torrential rains, but he felt certain it would pass. He felt he was making his contribution by enduring Davis. He would be among the first Negroes to graduate and go on to be one of the few working at Rodman Advertising.

Reggie and Betty continued to escape scrutiny as they met for brief encounters in secluded places. His feelings for her continued to grow. One day when they were about to go their separate ways, Reggie held her tightly and said, "I love you and I wonder if there is ever any future for us?"

Betty became flustered. She quickly pulled away.

"I don't know what the future holds. I wish things were different but let's enjoy ourselves now and not worry about the future," Betty said, while she looked in every direction except into Reggie's eyes. Reggie felt limp. She could have at least said she loved me too, he mourned. After that discussion, Betty began to make excuses about why she was unable meet him. One day he saw her on campus holding hands and engaged in animated conversation with a white boy. Reggie was sure she saw him. It was the day before their next planned rendezvous and Reggie was looking forward to questioning her about the guy. Betty did not show up, and for the first time did not send a note explaining why.

Reggie returned to his room, turned on his favorite album and thought about Mona.

He wanted to tell someone that Betty was no good but there was no safe anchor to lay that burden. His mind traveled back to Alfred's statement: "There will be no open arms welcoming you to white heaven." Maybe there is some truth to that statement, he wondered. Whenever he encountered Betty on campus, she would avoid both closeness and eye contact.

The rest of Reggie's sophomore and junior years followed a pattern. Dr. Thorn continued to advise him and he continued to make the grades to maintain his scholarship. He continued to participate in the Centennial Committee and was invited to go to the student union with members after meetings, but that was the limit of their social interactions.

None of this was known to Nancy and Sandra. They only saw him with the group in the student union so they assumed a deeper relationship and continued to distance themselves from him. Harry was still the best friend Reggie had, but Harry had fallen in love and spent much of his time with his new girlfriend. Summers were spent working at Rodman in Chicago, which Reggie always looked forward to. The brief periods at the end of summer and Christmas were spent in Smoky Mountain, and they became more and more of an obligation.

Beverly seldom spent more than a few days when she came home, and when she and Reggie were there at the same time, he only got to speak to her briefly on the telephone. She had decided if her parents did not welcome Deborah in their home, she would minimize her visits.

After finishing the two years at Lane College, Alfred had taken a job in sales with Universal Life, the Negro-owned insurance company. He seldom showed up when Reggie contacted him when he was in town and arranged a meeting. When he did show up, he was always rushed and claimed he had another appointment. After a while, Reggie stopped calling him.

Reggie was at the bus station on his way back to school the summer between his junior and senior years when he bumped into Arnold, whose bus arrived from Washington just as Reggie was about to board his. Arnold walked up behind Reggie and tapped him on the shoulder. Reggie turned around and grabbed Arnold's hand and began to shake it. Arnold hugged him.

"Well, what have you been up to in our nation's capital?" Reggie asked. He noticed Arnold's straight hair was much longer than he remembered and that he had grown a beard.

"Everything my brother, we are in high gear preparing for the revolution when our folks will take over. You need to come visit me in D.C. I could show you a lot. How are things at Davis?" Arnold asked.

"I'm doing fine. I still work at the advertising agency in Chicago during the summers. Oh, by the way, I was selected to work on the Centennial Planning Committee at Davis," Reggie proudly announced.

"Are they going to celebrate the day they let you in?" Arnold asked sarcastically.

"I don't know," Reggie said as he began to feel angry. "We haven't gotten that far in the plan."

"We!" Arnold shouted. "Brother you had better check yourself. There ain't no 'we' at Davis. You are beginning to sound like a white man covered in black paint. Is that the agenda of integration? Watch out, brother, you could get all messed up in the head."

"Don't worry about me. I know my way home," Reggie said. He felt like telling Arnold to kiss him where the good Lord split him but the bus was about to leave so he grabbed his bag and told Arnold he would see him next time. Arnold shouted, "You better get ready for the revolution. It's coming."

29

Before his Senior year, Reggie made his usual stopover in Smoky Mountain on his way back to school after a summer in Chicago. This was the first time he had seen Doug since his honorable discharge from the Army. Doug had returned to Smoky Mountain all geared up for the white collar job he was sure he would get. His travels to Germany and around Europe, and the tall tales of his life in the Army , increased his popularity. He took full advantage of this until a pointed shot gun sent him walking down the aisle and saying "I do" to Doris McKinley.

Their first child was due at the end of the year. After failing to succeed in acquiring the respectable job he had hoped for, Doug went to work alongside his father at Sleep Well Manufacturing. He tried to put on a happy face to hide his disappointment at reaching this point in his life with a crummy job, a woman he didn't care anything about outside the bedroom and a child he had not counted on. Reggie saw through his front and tried to encourage him to enroll at Lane College on a part-time basis and get a degree. He told Reggie he was now a family man with a wife, a house, and soon a child to take care of. That would not give him time to play school anymore.

Mr. and Mrs. Morton were disappointed that Doug was not able to get a better job and angry with Doris, who they claimed planned her pregnancy to get Doug to marry her and make her respectable. She was very attractive, but many men in the community claimed fond memories of her. Doris knew that there was no love for her in the Morton's home, which created a challenge for Doug. He had to go out and rent a house which he could not afford. He felt caught between two feuding families that needed to be brought together, but he was determined to rise to the occasion and regain the pride of his mother. Whenever emotions boiled over, he showed his ability to be rational with his mother and patient with Doris, qualities that eluded him when he was younger, but had developed in the Army. When the baby was born, things changed. Mrs. Morton loved the child so much she became tolerant of Doris.

Reggie wished he could do something to change his brother's life. He thought about all the things Mr. Sanders said about Negroes. He knew Doug was no hoodlum focused on crime and dependency. He was a man who served his country, expecting the rewards of service, faced the disappointment of not getting it, and went on to assume his responsibility like a man.

Mrs. Morton had heard a rumor that additional teachers would be needed in the fall at Central High, the previously all-white school. She had her heart set on the job for Reggie since they had begun to place Negro teachers in white schools. She thought her son would be a great role model for Negro students attending Central High because of his experience at Davis. She was hoping this would give her an edge over those forces out of Chicago.

She made her case to Reggie, telling him how much everybody looked forward to his being among the first Negro teachers in their integrated schools. She brought in Rev. Bailey, who reminded Reggie that his success at Davis was on the backs of other Negroes who endured much so he would have the opportunity. Reggie felt cornered and that made him feel angry and guilty. But he promised Mrs. Morton that he would enroll in the necessary courses to qualify for a teacher's license and would apply for the job, but he was not convinced he would make the decision to come home and teach. This was not a choice he would let his mentors in Chicago know he was considering.

Reggie remained on campus during spring break to help with planning the Centennial Celebration kick-off. He was so proud he was willing to make any sacrifice. All seniors had been issued their caps and gowns just before spring break to be worn during the opening ceremony which was scheduled two days after classes resumed. Reggie was beside himself. He tried them on in his room and marched in front of the mirror. Even though graduation was two months away, he felt he had arrived. He was going to be introduced during the celebration as one of the members of the Student Planning Committee and the thought caused him to break out in pimples. He wished his parents could be there to see him. It would be more recognition than when he received his degree. "I am now a Davis man, stamped and approved, and not many Negroes can make that claim," he said as he looked in the mirror.

He could not sleep the night before the celebration. It was like waiting for Santa Claus. At the appointed time the next morning, he donned his cap and gown and found his place in the procession. He was nervous and marched with his head held stiff, looking straight ahead. When his name was called during introductions, his legs felt weak but he stood proudly. He was glad it only took a few seconds, otherwise he might have fallen. He was surprised the audience clapped for him just as they did for others. "This is a day I will always remember," he kept mumbling under his breath.

He walked off the stage and into Harry who was waiting at the bottom of the steps, extending his hand and offering congratulations. Reggie beamed. Someone was there who could attest to his story. They started walking back to the dorm, Reggie still in his cap and gown. Harry announced that he and Linda Elam were getting married in August and he wanted Reggie to be his best man. Reggie searched for extra oxygen to take a deep breath. He had never thought about something like that.

"Congratulations, my friend, are you really serious? I would be glad to hold your hand through the ordeal. Are you sure you have sowed all your wild oats or do you intend to continue farming?" Reggie asked.

What a day this has been, he thought. He wondered if this could be what greets you at the end of the road after you have shown you can take it.

"I'm ready. Linda is the one for me. I've known for a long time and when she accepted my proposal, I knew awkward Harry who never had his father's charm was one lucky son-of-a-gun. Mother loves her and now that you have agreed to be my best man, everything is settled. Thanks Reggie. Let me go tell Linda."

30

THE EXCITEMENT OF THE CENTENNIAL KICK-OFF CELEBRATION DAY GRIPPED Reggie and sustained him through the remaining weeks and the very, very final exams. When he returned to the dorm after his last test, he found the letter from the Board of Education in Smoky Mountain. He had forgotten that he applied for a job there. They offered him a teaching job in civics at Central High with a salary of $4,500. He threw his hands over his head, looked up at the ceiling and shouted, "yes! yes!" It was his first job offer and the salary was more money than he could imagine. He began to anticipate his first car and driving around the neighborhood, slowing down to a crawl in front of the Townsend's house.

The following week he received a letter from Dr. Hunt telling him Rodman would not be able to offer him a job because of lost business; however, Mrs. Sanders had acquired a position for him at Woodlawn Foods as an administration assistant in marketing at a salary of six thousand dollars at the firm her family once owned. When he saw the salary, he dropped onto the bed and said, "Hey Arnold, match this if you can?" But his elation was short lived. He did not understand why he did not get an offer from Rodman. Everyone seemed so impressed with him and surely he could be given an entry level management position. The agency had five such slots. It would have been so easy to go to work there. Now, he would be faced with a completely new environment and new people to impress.

He didn't want to disappoint Mrs. Sanders or have her think he did not appreciate all she had done for him. But, he thought, if he accepted the teaching job, Mrs. Sanders would probably be the one person in Chicago who would understand. After all, she was the one who complimented him on that choice the first day they met.

The graduation announcements arrived. They read:

Davis University announces its one hundredth commencement exercise on Sunday, June Sixth, Nineteen hundred sixty three at Three O'clock in the afternoon at B. Peckman stadium, 1300 Clifton Avenue, Danville, Tennessee.

Reggie read it over and over again with tears crawling down his cheeks. Maybe it was all worth it, he thought. "I am without a doubt a Davis man, just like the governor, one of the state senators and the mayor of Smoky Mountain. There are only four other Negroes who can make that claim. I guess I am sort of a historical figure. I took it and I made it."

He immediately mailed the announcements off to his mother to send out as she saw fit. At the same time, he informed her of his two job offers. He tried to put a positive spin on Rodman's decision not to offer him a position. He told her Mrs. Sanders had found a better position for him in her family's company.

When Mrs. Morton received the announcements, she jumped up and down, shouting, "Thank you Jesus! Thank you Jesus for bringing my son through Davis." She thought about that day in the kitchen when they were discussing the Brown decision. She told him an education in an integrated school would give him privileges she and his father had never dreamed of having and now the forecast was about to come true and she was alive to see it. "Hallelujah!" she shouted.

The joy subsided when she remembered what he said about the job offers. She knew that was bound to happen and she had done everything she could to influence the decision. It hurt that he might not return home, but it was more painful to think he would probably fall into the web of those misguided folks in Chicago. They could make him forget where he came from. "Dear Lord, from whence all help cometh, my faith looks up to you. I know you will guide Reggie and bring him home to us," she prayed.

She immediately saw through Reggie's account of what happened to the job at Rodman. She thought maybe this was the Lord's way of opening his eyes to what he was in for if he decided to go to Chicago.

She wrote back telling Reggie that Doug, Doris and Doug, Jr. would be coming to the graduation along with her and his father. They would be arriving early that morning and would be returning to Smoky Mountain after graduation. Reggie was excited to know the whole family was coming. He really looked forward to seeing his nephew and giving the family a tour of the campus that he would always be able to claim as his own. It was sobering, however, when he remembered that the decision about which job offer to accept was still lurking out there haunting him. His mother would be anxiously waiting to hear the word. He knew she had been sprucing up his room in anticipation of his arrival.

Graduation day finally arrived and found Reggie full of energy with little rest. He was operating on adrenaline after tossing all night thinking about the momentous day and the weighty decision hanging over him. "First things first," he declared and jumped out of bed, laid out his suit, shirt and tie and spread out his cap and gown on the empty bed before charging to the shower. Around one o'clock, the old Mercury pulled up in front of the dorm with a group of proud people. Mr. Morton was wearing his blue suit and sporting a new haircut. He stepped out of the car as if he had only been in it for a few minutes while everybody stretched and yawned.

He had been silent during the drive. There were times when he wanted to laugh out loud when he remembered the guys on his job who kept referring to him as the father of an "egghead" when he told them about Reggie's graduation. That was the best comparison to an egg he had ever heard, he told them. He thought about all those long hours and humiliating demands he endured over the years in that factory and decided Reggie's graduation showed his bosses his endurance had a purpose. He felt ashamed of his earlier doubts about the Brown decision and could not believe the wildfire speed of the Civil Rights Movement spreading before his very eyes. It certainly was not happening any time too soon, but he was unsure how long it would last or what the ultimate result would be. One thing was certain, however; Reggie would not have to depend on that factory for a job like Doug. Today, that was victory enough for him.

Mrs. Morton nervously pressed her hand over her dress to make sure there were no wrinkles and instructed Doug to go and tell Reggie they had arrived. Doug handed Doug, Jr. over to Doris and charged into the dorm. Doris held Doug Jr. on her hip while she stood behind the Mortons constantly shoving Doug Jr.' s hand away from her hair. She was wearing a pink two-piece suit that flaunted what she considered her greatest asset, a stunning figure that made men dream. It made her feel as important as the rest of the family that day.

Reggie and Doug charged out of the dorm, busting in laughter as if their team had just won a game. Reggie saw Doug, Jr. and immediately took him from Doris and began kissing him. It suddenly occurred to him he was an uncle and a possible role model. It was exciting until he remembered Rev. Bailey's speech about the obligation of those who would be the first in their families to go to college. Reggie figured Doug Jr. would watch what he did with his life.

Like a proud father, Reggie took the family on a tour and gave them a vivid description of the centennial kick-off ceremony with emphasis on how the audience applauded him. As they walked around, Mrs. Morton reached for Mr. Morton's hand and squeezed it while tears welled in her eyes. Doug became quiet as he walked with his son in one arm and his wife's hand in the other. The family was awed by the beautiful campus and the sea of white families surrounding them. They all seemed to realize Reggie had succeeded in a world they did not know, and having seen that world, they felt even more outside of it.

At the end of the tour, Mrs. Morton asked Reggie had he made a decision about the job at Central High. He told her that he had not and he wanted to discuss it with Mrs. Sanders before deciding, and he was going to speak to her after graduation. He also said that he would not be leaving with them because the Centennial Committee was having a party for the graduating seniors in addition to him having to meet with the Sanders.

When Reggie's name was called to receive his degree and he walked across the stage, there was the usual applause from the audience. Mrs. Morton remembered the little baby with bright eyes who was quick to smile and who was always in some mischief, but who didn't want to miss a day of school and who brought home those great report cards. He was her baby. Tears rolled down her cheeks. Doug shouted, "Yeah, Yeah," in addition to his applause. Mr. Morton sat like a stone, determined not to show his emotions.

Following the ceremony, Reggie took his family to meet Dr. Thorn. She was flattered and said, "You must be proud of Reginald. He has been a wonderful student here and I am going to miss him." She looked at Reggie, reached for his hand, shook it and said,

"I will be very disappointed if I don't hear from you after today." Reggie looked at her, hoping his eyes would say what his heart felt, but he could not articulate.

After furrowing his eyebrows to hold the tears, he managed to say, "I will never forget you and I will definitely keep in touch."

He shook her hand again and held it for a while, speechless. Dr. Thorn pulled away, patted him on the shoulder and waved the family good-bye. As soon as Reggie turned around, Harry was there with Mr. and Mrs. Sanders. There were mutual introductions and then Mrs. Sanders said in jest, "I hope you don't mind that we have captured your son. He is such a bright and affable young man."

"He is a grown man now and can determine who captures him," Mrs. Morton said in a less than friendly tone. Mr. Sanders stepped in and invited the Mortons to join them for lunch. Mrs. Morton apologized, in a more cordial manner, and explained that they were driving back to Smoky Mountain that afternoon and would not have time for lunch.

"I am so sorry. We were looking forward to spending some time with you. Please say you will visit us in Chicago," Mrs. Sanders said.

"Thank you for the invitation. I hope one day we will be able to," Mrs. Morton said as the Morton family walked away.

"We look forward to your arrival in Chicago," Mrs. Sanders called out to Reggie. Reggie nodded his head and said, "Thanks for everything." Mrs. Morton bristled, but decided Reggie had not had a chance to speak to her, which is why he responded the way he did.

Mr. Sanders reached over and clasped his wife's hand, threw his arm around Harry's shoulders and, with all the energy he could muster to disguise his contempt, said, "Don't worry, honey. You have done a good thing."

As the last word escaped his lips, Mrs. Sanders felt as if a hypnotic drug had just kicked in, and with unyielding trust and devotion gleaming in her eyes, said, "I believe you, dear." Harry looked straight ahead, batting his eyes to hold back his tears of joy.

The historical day was beginning to wind down. It was time for Reggie to bid his family good-bye. He hugged them all, but held on to his mother for an extended period as if they were saying a final farewell. Reggie stood watching as the car drove out of sight. It had been a great day, but he was glad it was over. He was tired and could only think of going to his room and collapsing, but decided to check his mailbox for the last time. A letter was there with unfamiliar handwriting. The cancellation stamp indicated that it was from Smoky Mountain, which raised his curiosity. He opened it immediately and began reading while walking to his room. It read,

Dear Reginald,

I was really happy to receive the announcement of your graduation. Congratulations. This must be a time of great pride for you and your family. I remember how excited you were the morning after the Supreme Court handed down the Brown decision and how much you seemed to be interested in taking advantage of the new law. Well, you can think of yourself as a pioneer. You probably endured much pain as you made your way through those four years. I am sure you were not welcomed in many aspects of life on campus and there were times when you must have felt alone and yearned for the nurturing environment of a Historically Black College, but you stuck it out and that is the story those coming after you need to hear. I hope your will and determination to succeed at Davis gave you a deeper appreciation of your roots. It's often hard to remain loyal to your culture when all the rewards around you are for conforming to another. But there lies another challenge for someone like you, Reginald. Your culture now includes four years at an integrated school. Well, the mission of a pioneer is seldom a smooth path.

I am really proud of you and wish you the best as you move into the next phase of your life. Please keep in touch and let me know how you are doing.

Sincerely,
Sara Wright

Reggie placed the letter on his desk, went to bed and tossed and turned most of the night. The next morning he looked out the window and noticed that it was a warm day with overcast skies, the kind of day you don't mind, but wish the skies were clearer. He stood at the window trying to recapture all the good times and bad times at Davis. He felt sad, victorious and confused. Finally, he gathered his things, packed them in that old suitcase he was determined to replace with his first paycheck, and headed for the Greyhound bus station. He stood outside the station for a while, thinking how excited he was the first day he arrived there and how much his life had changed since that day. The bus was not due for an hour so he decided to have some breakfast. He ambled over to the restaurant counter, looked over the menu for a while and decided on a ham and egg sandwich, orange juice and a cup of coffee. There was a radio playing behind the counter. It was tuned to the all-Negro station out of Memphis. The disc jockey announced, "Ladies and gentlemen we have the St. Cecilia Glee Club from Booker T. Washington High School here today.

They will be singing the Negro National Anthem." Their harmonious voices began rolling through the airwaves. Reggie listened, for lack of something else to do, as they sang the first two stanzas, but the third grabbed his attention and he began to hum along as they sang,

God of our weary years, God of our silent tears, Thou who hast brought us thus far on the way; Thou who hast by Thy might led us in to the light; Keep us forever in the path, We pray Lest our feet stray from the places our God, where we met thee; Lest, our hearts drunk with the wine of the world, we forget Thee; Shadowed beneath Thy hand may we forever stand, True to our God, true to our native land.

It was fifteen minutes to departure time. Reggie was feeling anxious. He decided he needed to move around and walked out to the platform to wait. The sound of the bus entering the station brought him some relief. He was first in line when the driver was ready to take tickets. He boarded and found a seat next to a window and sat back for the ride. He again watched the fast-moving images on the landscape come into view and disappear as the bus trailed down the highway.

Somewhere along the way he fell asleep and every now and then he would awake and look out the window as if he would find the answer to life's mysteries, or at least his place in the saga. The last time he awoke the driver was saying, "Ladies and gentlemen, you have reached downtown Chicago."

ABOUT THE AUTHOR

Ernest Jones grew up in the segregated South during the 1940s and 50s and went away to a private college in the North during the Civil Rights Movement. After college he took a job in the Anti-Poverty program and joined a team responsible for developing and implementing a training program for students from urban areas who dropped out of school. The program was sponsored by IBM. He went on to become Director of The Advertising Consortium for Training minorities in New York City. He developed Grey Advertising's first Affirmative Action Program. As Chief of Conciliation for New York City Commission on Human Rights, he negotiated forty-five Affirmative Action agreements with Fortune 500 corporations.

In the 1980s, he relocated to Washington, D.C. and consulted with the Equal Employment Opportunity Commission in developing its Rapid Charge Processing system and with the U. S. Department of Housing and Urban Development in establishing their Systemic Discrimination Complaints program. He founded the U.S. Coast Guard's program for recruiting minorities at Historically Black Colleges and Universities and served as the service's manager of Hispanic program. He developed the New York City Health and Hospitals Corporation's Multicultural program and was one of the founders of "Competitive Edge," an organization dedicated to improving opportunities for minority- and women-owned businesses. He has also served as Co-chair of the Racial Justice Initiative, Mission and Social Justice Commission and the MSJ Common Table at the Riverside Church in New York City.

Printed in the United States
118856LV00003B/10-12/P

9 780980 238037